KU-632-452

Other books by Ben Miller

The Night I Met Father Christmas

The Boy Who Made the World Disappear

The Day I Fell Into a Fairytale

How I Became a Dog Called Midnight

Diary of a Christmas Elf

THE
DAY
I FELL
INTO A
FAIRYTALE

BEN MILLER

THE DAY I FELL INTO A FAIRYTALE

Illustrated by
Daniela Jaglenka Terrazzini

SIMON & SCHUSTER

First published in Great Britain in 2020 by Simon & Schuster UK Ltd
This paperback edition first published in 2021

Text copyright © Passion Projects Limited 2020
Illustrations copyright © Daniela Jaglenka Terrazzini

This book is copyright under the Berne Convention.
No reproduction without permission.
All rights reserved.

The rights of Ben Miller and Daniela Jaglenka Terrazzini to be identified as the
author and illustrator of this work respectively has been asserted by them
in accordance with sections 77 and 78 of the Copyright,
Designs and Patents Act, 1988.

5 7 9 10 8 6 4

Simon & Schuster UK Ltd
1st Floor, 222 Gray's Inn Road
London
WC1X 8HB

www.simonandschuster.co.uk

Simon & Schuster Australia, Sydney
Simon & Schuster India, New Delhi

A CIP catalogue record for this book is available from the British Library.

PB ISBN 978-1-4711-9244-9
eBook ISBN 978-1-4711-9245-6
Audio ISBN 978-1-4711-9535-8

This book is a work of fiction. Names, characters, places and incidents are either
the product of the author's imagination or are used fictitiously. Any resemblance to
actual people living or dead, events or locales is entirely coincidental.

Printed and bound by CPI Group (UK) Ltd, Croydon, CR0 4YY

To my parents, Mick and Marion Miller,
who gave me my love of reading

Prologue

Suddenly there it was. A fresh mound of earth, the size of a molehill, right in the middle of the common.

Only it wasn't a molehill.

Not that anyone saw it form. It was the dead of night and a storm was raging, so the villagers were all safely tucked up in their beds, with their curtains shut and their electric blankets on.

But as they slept, the little mound of earth started to grow. And as the wind howled, and the rain lashed, it grew larger and larger. Higher and higher it rose, until it was the size of a haystack.

Lightning crackled in the sky, and thunder rolled out across the valley. The mound of earth began to shake and its peak trembled and quivered, until suddenly a gleaming white enamel flagpole popped out of the top!

Up and up climbed the flagpole, rising out of the ground like a beanstalk in a fairytale. Once it had reached its full height, it paused before it too began to quiver and shake. Because the flagpole was just the beginning.

Cracks crazed their way across the common, as the turf began to warp and split, and something truly enormous began to emerge.

A roof. A colossal, aluminium roof! Up and up it buckled, pushed by the cinder block walls emerging from the ground beneath it. Earth tumbled away and, like a giant rising from its slumber, an entire building began to rise. Girders popped into place, door frames righted themselves, and sheets of plate glass found their groove. Once everything was in place, the entire structure fell slient.

Still the rain lashed down, washing everything clean.

Then the heavy grey clouds cleared, and a full moon shone bright as a penny. The wind calmed and the rain stopped.

In a nearby field, a cock crowed. It was morning now, and across the valley the pale dawn sky brightened to blue. Soon, the first rays of sunlight were chasing across the still-sleeping village. And there, at the bottom of the hill, smack dab in the middle of the common, what had started as a mound of earth no bigger than a molehill, was now a brand-new supermarket.

A breeze fluttered, and at the top of the flagpole, a maroon-and-gold flag unfurled. On it was a single word.

Grimm's.

'Still the rain lashed down, washing everything clean.'

Chapter One

L ana was bored. It had finally stopped raining, but she had no one to play with.

Usually her older brother, Harrison, made up the most brilliant games: Knights of the Round Table, for example, or Soldiers and Zombies. But ever since he'd started senior school, Harrison had changed.

He had become Serious. Even though he was on holiday too, all he did was sit in his bedroom and work.

After breakfast, when Lana had knocked to see if he wanted to play in the treehouse, he had closed the door in her face without saying a word.

Now, ten minutes later, she had returned to check if he'd changed his mind, but found a large sign on his door that read:

VERY IMPORTANT HOMEWORK IN PROGRESS. DO NOT DISTURB.

I'm sure that's really aimed at our parents, thought Lana. *I bet he's secretly hoping I ask him to play again . . .*

This time she decided not to knock, and found

Harrison sitting at his desk, concentrating hard on the books and papers in front of him.

'Didn't you see the sign?' he said, without looking up. 'What do you want?'

'I was just wondering if you'd like to play a game?'

Harrison still didn't look up.

'We can play whatever you want. Boxers. Pirates. Police. I don't mind!'

Harrison sighed and put down his pen. He took off his glasses and pinched the bridge of his nose. It was something Lana had seen their father do and clearly Harrison thought

it made him look grown-up and important.

'Lana,' he said. 'I don't have time to play games anymore. Do you know what an oxbow lake is?'

Lana didn't.

'It's a special kind of lake that's formed when a river becomes too twisty. Anyway, I'm busy reading all about them.'

'Maybe after that?' she offered.

Harrison frowned. 'Well, after oxbow lakes I need to learn about Archimedes.'

Lana looked blankly at her brother.

'He's from Ancient Greece,' said Harrison. 'He's basically the first scientist.'

'Sounds fun,' Lana said, which it most definitely did not. She tried her best not to look disappointed. It didn't work.

Harrison's face softened. A part of him

did miss their adventures. For a start, Lana always threw herself into whatever game they played. There were few police officers so committed to maintaining law and order, and few zombies as determined to destroy human civilisation as his little sister.

'Sorry,' he said. 'We'll do something soon, I promise.'

But Lana knew that wasn't true.

It was time for drastic measures. Whenever she really needed cheering up, there was one place Lana loved to go: the dressing table where her mother kept her perfumes. Lana wasn't really allowed to play with them, but there was something so magical about all those bottles, with their strange names and fancy shapes, that she found them hard to resist. So, she snuck into her parents' bedroom and surveyed the entire collection, examining each one, until her eyes landed on a tall vial made from crimson cut-glass, with the word *Enchantment* printed across the middle in swirling gold letters. She carefully removed the lid and took a deep sniff.

Suddenly her mother's voice rang out very close by. 'Oh, thank goodness! The rain's stopped!'

Lana panicked, fumbling with the lid and accidentally squirted the perfume into her left eye. 'Ow!' she cried, burying her face in the crook of her elbow.

Her mother put her head round the door. She frowned and sniffed the air. 'What's that smell? Is it perfume?'

'I can't smell anything,' said Lana. She quickly hid the bottle behind her back. Her eye was smarting and a tear rolled down her left cheek.

'Are you okay?' asked her mother in concern.

Then it dawned on Lana: her mother thought she was upset.

'Harrison won't play with me,' she said, quickly making a sad face.

Her mother nodded thoughtfully. 'I know,' she said. 'He's worried about his exams.'

'But why?' asked Lana. 'He's only in his first year of senior school. Exams are AGES away.'

'He just wants to be prepared,' said her mother, with a note of worry in her voice.

'You know what he's like.'

'I miss him.'

'Oh, Lana. I'm sorry.' Her mother opened her arms and gave Lana a big cuddle. Lana felt her tears become real. 'Your brother's growing up. That's what happens.'

Now that she had started crying, Lana found she couldn't stop.

'Let's go out and cheer you up,' said her mother decisively, determined to change her daughter's mood. 'Why don't you come to Grimm's with me?'

'Where?'

'Oh, it's very exciting,' said her mother earnestly. 'Overnight a supermarket seems to have sprung up from nowhere on the common! I saw it on my walk this morning.'

Lana sighed with disappointment. 'It's the

school holidays,' she said. 'We're meant to do *fun* things. And supermarkets *aren't* fun.'

'Come on,' replied her mother. 'I'll buy you a treat.'

Lana's ears pricked up. 'What sort of treat? A book?' She might not be able to have fun adventures with Harrison, but if she could find a new book she could at least read about far-off lands or daring escapes.

'Yes, if that's what you want. Now, I'm going downstairs to tell your father that we're going out. Hopefully, by the time you join me, all my perfumes will be back where they belong.'

Lana tried to look innocent.

'Including the one you're hiding behind your back,' said Lana's mother with a breezy smile.

Chapter Two

I f there was one thing to say about Little Hilcot, the village where Lana lived, it was this: it never changed. As they drove down the hill from their cottage, everything she saw was achingly familiar. There was the same old red post box, standing sentry outside the village shop, and there was the same old row of crooked houses, threatening to collapse onto the tiny village school. Last of all came Hilcot House, with its high yew hedge, where every summer the Gatcombe family hosted the village fete.

But as they made the turn out onto the common, Lana could scarcely believe her eyes. Her mother was right: there, where yesterday Lana was sure there had been nothing but grass, was the most enormous new supermarket. A fresh tarmac road swept them off the lane and through a neat brick arch, into a colossal car park, with trees and shrubbery planted in orderly fashion.

'Well, what do you think?' asked Lana's mother, parking in one of the newly marked-out bays and turning off the engine.

'Where did all this come from?' asked Lana, gazing up at the shiny new building.

'I don't know. I suppose they must have been building it through all the bad weather, when everyone was indoors? Although how they did it with no one noticing . . .' Lana's mother trailed off, looking puzzled. 'Anyway, shall we go and take a look around?'

They both climbed out of the car and headed to the entrance. Lana's mother unhitched the first in an enormous line of brand-new shopping trolleys, and swished in through the automatic doors.

By the time Lana caught up with her, she was already loading her trolley with bumper packs of toilet roll.

'Look at this!' her mother cooed. 'Forty-eight rolls for the price of twenty-four! And it's three-ply. We need to snap this up while we've still got the chance. As soon as word gets out, this place will be rammed!'

'That's great,' replied Lana, trying to sound enthusiastic. 'But do we really need that much toilet roll?'

'What's this?' asked her mother in an awed voice. 'Buy nineteen boxes of aluminium foil and get the twentieth free? That's unbelievably good value.'

'Can I go and find the book section?' asked Lana.

'That can't be right . . .' muttered her mother, in a world of her own. 'Thirty-six bags of barbecue briquettes for the price of thirty? I wonder if that's a misprint.'

Lana was about to say that they didn't have a barbecue, but thought better of it. And while her mother continued shopping, she quietly slipped away . . .

Grimm's, it seemed, was enormous. After wandering aimlessly through a huge Fruits and Vegetables section, Lana found herself marooned in a never-ending row of Baked Goods that finally led to Jams and Preserves, which merged into Biscuits and Cereals, before making her way through the Frozen Ready Meals aisle and finding herself back at . . . Fruits and Vegetables. The shelves and fridges that bordered the aisles were double her height and Lana began to lose hope of ever finding the book section.

She thought about asking for directions, but not only were there no other customers; she couldn't see any staff either. The tills were empty and there was no one behind the deli; the pharmacy and the café were silent. For one brief moment Lana thought she spotted someone stacking the freezers, but it turned out to be her mother, loading her overflowing trolley with boxes of frozen pizza.

Lana was about to give up her book search, when she heard a peculiar scuffling noise that seemed to be coming from an aisle towards the far end of the store.

'Fittlesticks!' rasped a high, nasal voice. 'Rickety snickety fittlesticks!'

Curious, Lana crept forward. There, standing on tiptoe, arms outstretched, struggling to place a large red leather-bound book on a high shelf, was an extremely odd-looking man. He was roughly Lana's height, but looked much older – as old as her grandpa – and he was dressed in a maroon boiler suit with a smart gold trim. His eyes were beady and brown, his nose and ears were enormous, and his large, bald head was speckled with warts.

'Well, don't just stand there, child!' he barked at her. 'Help me!'

Lana leapt forward and placed her hands on the wide spine of the book, either side of the man's. His fingernails were long and yellow.

'Push!' strained the little old man. 'Harder!'

Lana focused all her effort, but the book was extraordinarily heavy. Before she really knew what was happening, she toppled backwards, and found herself pinned to the floor, with the book sprawled open across her chest.

'You dropped it!' he spat.

'Sorry,' said Lana, squirming out from underneath. 'I did try my best.'

As she spoke, her eye caught one of the illustrations. It was of a witch, with a long nose and a sharp chin, surrounded by a tangled forest.

'No peeking,' snarled the little old man, snatching the book. His face was level with hers, and Lana could see tiny white bristles on the end of his nose. 'I'm putting it on a high shelf, away from nosy children like you.'

He was so defensive that Lana instantly wanted to know more about the book.

'Why does it need to be out of reach?' she asked. 'What's in it?'

'Fairytales,' replied the little old man,

hugging the book to his chest, as if he was worried that Lana might try to take it from him.

Fairytales? Now Lana was *really* interested! 'Can I see it?' she asked. 'I'm allowed to buy a book as a treat, and I love fairytales.'

'Not like these you don't,' he said, frowning at her. 'These are proper fairytales, centuries old, much too scary for you. You should give that one a go instead.' He pointed to a dull-looking picture book on the lowest shelf. 'It's called *The Little Tugboat Who Tried*. A big ship breaks down and a little tugboat tries to pull it to shore. Except the big ship is very heavy, almost too heavy, for the little tugboat.'

'And what happens?' asked Lana.

'Well, he keeps trying,' said the little old man, 'and eventually he manages it.'

'Right,' said Lana, thinking that either the story wasn't very interesting or the man wasn't telling it quite right.

'Trust me,' he said, pushing Lana towards the picture book. 'You'll be much happier with this. Look, see? Lots of bright, friendly, safe pictures.'

He turned away from Lana and, standing on his tiptoes again, he hoisted the big red fairytale book onto the highest shelf he could reach. 'There, out of harm's way, that's better.' And, without another word, he disappeared out of the aisle and round the corner.

Lana waited for a moment, then, after a quick look around, she stretched up, pulled the red book down from the shelf and then hurried off to find her mother. If the little old man was so determined to keep the fairytales from her then they must be good.

As soon as Lana was gone, the man peered back round the corner, a tiny smile on his face.

'If you want a child to read something . . .' he whispered to himself. 'Tell her it's forbidden.'

'What on Earth have you got there?' asked her mother, at the checkout. There was no one at the till, but she had piled everything from her trolley high on the conveyor belt anyway.

'It's a book of fairytales,' said Lana, proudly. 'I'd like it as my treat, please.'

'Oh,' said Lana's mother, and sneezed six times in quick succession. 'Dust,' she croaked, and sneezed another eleven times. 'Are you sure this is for sale? It looks very old.'

'Ummm . . .' began Lana.

'Can I help you?' said a familiar voice, and Lana's mother jumped. There, sitting by the till, was the little old man. Except now he had a dark brown moustache and was wearing a white collared shirt with a maroon waistcoat, a maroon-and-gold necktie and a gold pillbox hat.

'Hello,' said Lana's mother. 'My daughter would like this book, but there's no price on it.'

'Oh, would she?' he asked, fixing Lana with a stare. 'How old is she?'

'Nine,' announced Lana.

'A young nine, or an old nine?'

'I'm sorry?' asked Lana's mother. 'What difference does that make?'

'These fairytales are not . . . *suitable* for a *young* nine. An *old* nine, maybe.'

'I see,' said Lana's mother, who really didn't like being told what she could or could not do by anyone, let alone strangers. She opened the book and skimmed the contents page. 'Oh yes,' she said, smiling. 'I used to love these stories when I was little. We'll take them, please.'

'As you wish, madam,' said the little old man. 'But don't say I didn't warn you. That'll be seventeen pence.'

Lana's mother looked at him blankly.

'But with your introductory discount,' he said, with a breezy smile, 'I can do it for eleven.'

Once Lana and her mother had left the supermarket, the little old man grinned to himself once more. 'And if you want an adult to buy something,' he muttered, 'make it cheap.'

Chapter Three

'Will you read to me?' Lana asked that evening, as her mother was tucking her into bed. 'From my new book of fairytales?'

'Of course,' said her mother, after she finished sneezing. 'Let's take a look at what we have . . . There's *Hansel and Gretel*. That's about a little boy and a little girl who get lost in the forest and find a house made of sweets.'

'That's so lucky!' said Lana. 'I'd love to find a house like that!'

'Ah, well, that's what Hansel and Gretel thought, only it was a trap.'

'A trap?' Lana's eyes widened.

'The house belongs to a witch, and when the children try to eat the sweets she captures them and they discover to their horror that, erm . . .' Lana's mother's voice trailed away.

'That what?' asked Lana.

'That she wants to eat them,' replied her mother briskly. 'It's a little bit of a scary story, so maybe let's not read *Hansel and Gretel*. How about this one, *Rumpelstiltskin*?'

'Rumpel-what?' asked Lana.

'*Rumpelstiltskin*. Here, there's a picture of him.'

Lana's mother turned the book round so Lana could take a look. There on the page was an old-fashioned picture of a familiar figure.

'That's the man from the supermarket!'

Lana's mother smiled. 'Hmmm, I suppose it does look a bit like him, doesn't it?'

'It's not *like* him,' pressed Lana. 'It *is* him.'

'Of course, dear,' said her mother dismissively. 'Anyway, here he is, spinning straw into gold.'

'Who's the girl?' asked Lana.

'The miller's daughter,' said her mother. 'From what I remember of the story, her father told the king that she could spin straw into gold, which was a lie. He was just showing off. So, the king locks the miller's daughter in a room full of straw and says if she hasn't spun it

all into gold by the morning, then he'll, erm . . .'
her mother's voice trailed away again.

'What will he do?' asked Lana.

'Er . . . kill her,' said her mother.

'Kill her!'

'Yes.' Her mother was beginning to
wonder if the man at the till had been right,
and the stories weren't suitable for Lana after
all. 'Look, maybe we should find a different
book to read tonight? Something a bit nicer?'

'But what happened to the miller's
daughter?' asked Lana.

'Well,' said her mother reluctantly, 'after
the king has gone, Rumpelstiltskin appears
and offers to spin all the straw into gold for
the girl, if she gives him her necklace. So,
she agrees, and he spins all the straw into
gold. But the next morning the king is so

impressed to see all the gold that, instead of letting the girl go, he locks her in a bigger room, with even more straw in it, and tells her to do it again.'

'Does the little old man come back?'

'Yes, he does, and he helps again, this time in return for a . . . ring. Yes, that's right, a ring.'

'And then does the king let her go?'

'Um, no actually,' her mother started to look a bit uncomfortable again. 'He locks her in an even bigger room, with an absolutely massive amount of straw, and tells her to do it again. This time she has nothing to give the little old man, so he asks for her . . . first born child in return,' said her mother, flicking through the pages. 'This isn't the nicest of stories either. Are you sure you don't want another book?'

'No! These all sound much more exciting than the things we usually read. What about this story?' asked Lana, pointing at a picture of a beautiful girl, asleep on a bed, with roses growing all around her.

'That's *Sleeping Beauty*,' said her mother. 'You must know that one?'

Lana shook her head, because she didn't.

'That was one of my favourites when I was little. I don't think it's scary . . . not that I can remember, anyway.'

'It sounds lovely! Please can we read it?' asked Lana.

'All right,' said her mother. 'I suppose we can read a little and see if it's suitable.'

And this . . . well, this is pretty much what she read:

Once there was a king and queen who very much hoped for a baby. But hope as they might, no baby came.

Soon they began to lose heart, and busied themselves with hobbies instead. The king organised archery competitions, while the queen took up wild swimming.

One day, when the queen was swimming in the castle moat, a strange red-eyed frog hopped out of the water and onto the bank.

'Great news!' chirruped the frog. 'Before the year is out, you and the king will have a child. Her name will be Briar Rose, and she will be everything your hearts desire.'

The frog, it seemed, was right, because several months later, the royal couple had a most beautiful baby girl.

The king and queen were so happy that they

decided to hold a feast to show Briar Rose off to the world.

They invited only the most important people in the kingdom, including the thirteen fairies.

Now, as everybody knows, fairies only eat off gold plates. But, as they were writing the invitations, the king realised they only had *twelve* gold plates and no time to get another, so instead of inviting all thirteen fairies, he only invited twelve.

Soon, the day of the party came, and after dinner each of the fairies came forward to give Briar Rose a gift.

'Darling, Briar Rose,' said the first fairy, 'I shall give you . . . beauty.'

'Briar Rose already has beauty,' said the second fairy, 'so I shall give her . . . wit.'

There were so many fairies that soon they were running out of gifts.

'Your baby already has beauty, wit, charm, grace, humility, bearing, exceptional leadership skills, excellent hand-eye co-ordination, an ear for music, a refreshing lack of self-pity and great hair,' said the twelfth fairy, 'so I shall give—'

'Stop right there!' boomed a voice, and everyone turned to see the thirteenth fairy in the doorway, looking very angry indeed.

'A little bird told me you were having a party without me,' she sneered at the king and queen. 'And what do you know? It's true!'

The king tried to explain, but the thirteenth fairy did not wish to hear excuses. Her brow furrowed, her upper lip snarled, and her eyes glowed as red as burning coals. Her black cloak billowed behind her and she began to rise up, growing taller and taller until she almost reached the ceiling. It really was a terrifying sight.

'Hoping for gifts, are you?!' she roared. 'Well, here's mine. On her fifteenth birthday, Briar Rose will prick her finger on a spindle and die!'

And, before anyone could stop her, she changed into a large red-eyed frog, then leapt out of the window.

For a moment, no one knew quite what to say. Then the queen burst into tears.

'Our darling daughter!' she wailed. 'What will become of you?'

But, luckily, the twelfth fairy had yet to give her gift. She had been going to give a remarkable ability to find lost socks, as that was pretty much all that was left, but now she saw her chance to do some good.

'I think I can help,' she said. 'The thirteenth fairy's magic is very strong, so I can't remove the curse, but I can soften it a little. On her fifteenth birthday, Briar Rose will indeed prick her finger on a spindle, but she will not die. Instead she will fall asleep for one hundred years–'

'Thank you! Thank you!' interrupted the queen with joy.

'What good is that?' said the king. 'One hundred years! When she wakes, we will all be dead!'

'If you'll let me finish,' said the twelfth fairy. 'When Briar Rose falls asleep, so will everyone else in the palace–'

'What?!' exclaimed the king. 'Everyone?'

'Yes,' said the twelfth fairy. 'Then, when she awakes, you will all wake with her.'

'You think there's going to be anything left of this place after one hundred years?' spluttered the king. 'This tablecloth alone is worth eighty ducats. That wall-hanging is worth five hundred. Everything will be stolen! The place will be overrun with thieves. I'll be lucky to wake up with my breeches on.'

'Ah, I've thought of that too,' said the twelfth fairy (who was, to be fair, getting a little impatient at being constantly interrupted). 'As soon as the castle falls into its slumber, a giant wall of thorns will grow all around it, protecting you all from anyone who tries to enter.'

'Seriously?' asked the king. 'That's the best you can do?'

'I'm sorry,' said the twelfth fairy, tartly. 'If someone's got a better idea, I'm eager to hear it.'

'Let's not anger another fairy, darling,' the queen said to her husband. 'One bad spell is quite enough to be going on with.'

The king harumphed and folded his arms but said nothing more.

'Thank you so much for helping us,' the queen said to the twelfth fairy. 'We gratefully accept your gift.'

'My pleasure,' said the twelfth fairy, still feeling slightly put out.

'Yes, thank you,' muttered the king, begrudgingly. 'But I intend to make sure Briar Rose doesn't prick her finger in the first place. From this moment forth, by royal decree, all spindles are banned. Each and every one of them must be destroyed!'

'What's a spindle?' asked Lana, looking up from the book.

'It's a pointy stick, basically. For spinning yarn,' said her mother.

'What's yarn?'

'Thread. You know, for making clothes.'

'So, if the king banned spindles . . . does that mean nobody had any clothes?'

'Erm, I'm not sure . . . Anyway, I think that's probably enough reading for one night.'

'But what happened?' protested Lana. 'Did it work? Banning spindles, I mean.'

'Lana, go to sleep. You can hear the rest at bedtime tomorrow.' And with that,

her mother closed the book, tucked Lana
under the covers, kissed her on the cheek,
and turned out the bedside light.

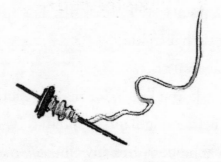

Chapter Four

The next morning, Lana woke early with only one thing on her mind: Briar Rose. Now that the thirteenth fairy had cursed her, and the king had banned spindles, she just had to know what happened next . . .

She reached for the book, determined to read it for herself. But her bedside table was empty except for her water glass, and there was no sign of it on her bookshelf either.

Mum must have taken it, she thought to herself. *She thinks it's too scary for me to read on my own.*

There was only one thing for it: she was going to have to steal the book back.

As quietly as she could, Lana tiptoed across the landing and poked her head round the door to her parents' bedroom. It was empty. She checked under the bed, on top of the chest of drawers, and on the shelves in her mother's clothes cupboard. But there was no sign of the book anywhere.

She was about to give up, when once again she caught sight of the bottle of *Enchantment* on her mother's dressing table. She couldn't resist. It wouldn't hurt to dab a drop on her wrists, she decided, like she sometimes saw her mother do. Besides, it might take her mind off Briar Rose.

Suddenly, she heard her father's voice in the hallway.

'Oh my goodness! Would you look at these prices!'

Once again, Lana scrambled around, trying to put the bottle back, accidentally pressing the nozzle. This time it squirted in her right eye, which immediately began to weep.

'Ow!' she cried, clasping her hands to her face.

'Poppet!' cooed her father, entering the room. 'What's the matter?'

Lana had no choice: she was going to have to pretend to be upset, just like she had with her mother.

'Mum's hidden my book,' said Lana, looking up at him with streaming eyes. Or rather, one streaming eye and one quite normal one.

'Oh, dear,' said her father, scooping her up in his arms. 'I'm sure she's just put it somewhere safe. Anyway, she's at work. I'm looking after you this morning.'

Disappointment flooded through Lana; now she would have to wait a whole day to find out where her mum had hidden her book. And, with Harrison busy studying again, another day of boredom stretched out ahead of her.

'Never mind, Lana,' said her father, producing a leaflet. 'Feast your eyes on this! I just found it on the doormat.'

Her vision was a bit blurry from all the fake

eye-rubbing, but even so, Lana could just about make out the name at the top: *Grimm's*.

'Look at these prices! Twenty-seven bottles of toilet cleaner for the price of twenty-six! Thirty-eight tubs of cocktail sticks for the price of thirty-seven!' His eyes lit up at the thought of such bargains. 'So, what do you say we go and check it out? It might cheer you up?'

Lana readily agreed. The strange supermarket, with its equally strange employee, was the most entertaining thing she'd come across for weeks.

When Lana and her father arrived at Grimm's a few minutes later, the car park was almost full to bursting. It seemed that news of a bargain travelled fast. Instead of parking right outside the store, they had to cruise round and round to try and find a space.

'These people can't all be from the village,' tutted her father. 'Haven't they got their own cut-price supermarkets to go to? Argh!'

As he spoke, an overloaded trolley lurched out onto the tarmac, forcing him to slam on the brakes.

'Mind where you're going!'

'Sorry!' called a bearded man from behind a mountain of kitchen roll. 'Didn't see you there!'

'Honestly,' said her father, under his breath. 'Does he really need all of that?'

'Perhaps he saw how cheap it was, and couldn't help himself?' suggested Lana, but her father didn't seem to pick up on the joke.

And that wasn't the only joke he didn't pick up on. As they crawled along the aisles, waiting their turn at the shelves, Lana invented a very funny game. Every time her father paused to study the price on something, Lana would sneak as much sugary food as she possibly could into the trolley. She risked two pints of chocolate milk, a family pack of Choco Pops and a bucket of chocolate-chip cookies.

It was only when he reached the checkout and started putting their shopping on the conveyor belt, that her father realised what Lana had been up to.

'Where did this chocolate log come from?' he asked accusingly. 'And what about this jar of chocolate spread?'

'Maybe the thirteenth fairy put them in there,' said Lana, helpfully.

'Who?'

'The thirteenth fairy. She wasn't invited to Briar Rose's party, so she didn't get any sweet treats.'

Lana's father narrowed his eyes.

'I see. Is this to do with your book of fairytales, by any chance?'

Lana nodded, trying not to giggle.

But her father wasn't amused. He took a shopping basket from beside the till and begin to fill it with Lana's stolen sugar. 'You need to put these back, right now, or there's going to be a Consequence.'

A Consequence, as Lana well knew, meant something bad.

'Like what?' she asked.

'Like no bedtime story,' said her father, who seemed to have a second sense for what Lana wanted most.

'But I want to find out what happens to Briar Rose!'

'Then you'd better be quick,' came the firm reply.

Which was how Lana found herself dragging a basket full of chocolate bars, cakes, biscuits and cereals around the corner of the Pet Food aisle, narrowly avoiding an elderly lady on a mobility scooter, who swerved wildly, running straight over the toe of the little old man. 'Oi!' he yelped, clasping his foot in pain. He was wearing his maroon boiler suit again and the moustache he'd had at the checkout was gone. 'Watch where you're going, you stupid old bat!'

But the elderly lady seemed not to hear, and trundled off down the aisle.

'Don't be so rude!' exclaimed Lana,

shocked at the little old man's reaction. 'Anyway, it wasn't her fault – it was mine.'

'Huh,' he grunted. 'I might have known.' A smile curled at the corner of his lips. 'Come to bring the book back, have you? I told you it was too scary.'

'Actually,' said Lana defiantly. 'I'm really enjoying it.'

'Really?' he asked, sounding surprised. 'Which story have you started with?'

'*Sleeping Beauty*,' said Lana.

'Oooh,' he said, smiling again. 'Where are you up to?'

'The thirteenth fairy has cast her curse and the king has destroyed the spindles.'

'Ah,' he said, nodding sagely. 'That explains it. That's just the set-up. You haven't got to the scary bit yet. Well, I'm sure when you do, you'll be bringing that book back, all right.'

And with that, he headed off down towards the Toys and Games aisle. Moving quickly, Lana chucked her basket in a nearby trolley and scurried after him.

'What scary bit?'

The little old man turned slowly.

'You *really* want to know?'

Lana nodded. He fished a well-thumbed red-leather booklet from the top pocket of his overalls, consulted it, then put it back.

'May I suggest you try the sherbet lemons?'

For a moment Lana couldn't understand what he could possibly mean, but then her eyes came to rest on something truly extraordinary. Smack dab in the middle of the toys were the biggest tubs of pick 'n' mix she had ever seen.

Lana frowned in confusion. Pick 'n' mix was one of her favourite things in the whole world, so she couldn't imagine how she hadn't noticed this HUGE selection yesterday. But there it was,  row after row of giant crystal-clear tubs, each and every one crammed full of the most delicious-looking sweets.

She took a step closer. Entranced, she lifted the nearest lid. An entire tub full of pear drops. She could almost feel the sharp crystallised sugar, scraping the roof of her mouth. She lifted the next lid. Jelly babies. She loved jelly babies!

'Found them yet?' grinned
the little old man.

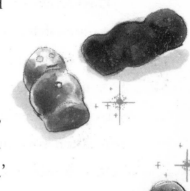

Lana shook her head.

'There, at the back.'

She tried to open the lid,
but it was just out of reach.

'Here, let me lift you up.'

And before Lana could protest,
he reached up under her arms,
and lifted her towards the lid of the tub.

'Go on,' he urged, straining under
her weight. 'Open it.'

His sharp hands were digging into
her armpits, so Lana quickly lifted the
lid. Unlike the other tubs, this one was
almost empty. Only a small cluster of
sherbet lemons clung to the bottom, like
hibernating beetles.

'Mmm, lovely,' she offered. 'Can I get down now?'

'Try one.'

Lana leant forward into the tub and tried to loosen a sweet with her finger, but it was no use. Then, suddenly, she was tumbling forward! The little old man was pushing her into the tub!

'Hey!' called Lana in alarm. 'Stop it!'

But it was too late! She threw out her hands ahead of her to brace her fall, but the bottom of the tub gave way like a trapdoor, and Lana found herself shooting down and round into a smooth-walled circular chute! Round and round she slid, until suddenly the chute plunged down, down, down into the darkness.

*'Lana found herself shooting down and round into
a smooth-walled circular chute!'*

Chapter Five

Lana clamped her eyes shut in terror as she whistled head first into the darkness, sure that she was about to smash into the ground at any second. Then, just when it felt as if she could go no faster, the chute began to spiral rapidly, slowing her little by little, until it yawned open, spitting her out onto what felt like an enormous soft cushion.

For a few minutes Lana lay there, flat on her back in the pitch black, her chest heaving, and her nose full of an odd aroma that she decided could only be cheese. She propped herself up onto her elbows. Was she still in one piece? She wiggled her fingers and toes. Nothing broken, so far as she could tell.

'Hello?' she said nervously. Her voice sounded flat and dull, as if she was in some sort of enclosed space. Checking that she was clear of the chute, she pushed herself up into a seated position. Cautiously, she crawled forward. *Thunk!* Her forehead hit something hard, and a door in front of her swung open to reveal a light so bright that she had to shield her eyes.

It was a candelabrum, ablaze with candles! Lana looked around. It appeared she was perched in a high cupboard, looking down onto an enormous circular old-fashioned kitchen. What's more, she was completely surrounded by cheeses. And the 'cushion' that had broken her fall was in fact an extremely ripe Camembert.

Where on earth was she?

'Hello?' Lana called. 'Is there anybody there?'

No one answered. A waft of sweet-smelling pastry curled at her nostrils and, looking down, she saw that immediately below her was a large table, laden with tray after tray of mouth-watering jam tarts. *Someone must be nearby*, she thought. *These look like they are straight out of the oven.*

And the jam tarts were just the beginning. As Lana looked around it seemed the entire kitchen was bursting with food: roast lamb with rosemary, fresh-baked pies with butter-glazed crusts, mouth-watering jellies seeded with fruit, cream horns with dollops of raspberry jam and a mountain of pillow-soft ham sandwiches.

She dangled one leg over the edge of the shelf. It was a long way down.

'Could someone help me?' she called.

It really was *very* quiet and still. Something wasn't right, she was sure of it. She felt a prickly feeling on her arm and pulled back her sleeve. Goosebumps.

'Hello?' she said again, a little more warily.

There was nothing for it; she would have to get down by herself. She turned, so that she was facing backwards, then lay down on her tummy to lower her legs onto the table.

At least that was what she planned to do. Unfortunately, kick, dangle and swing as she might, the table top was nowhere to be found. So, she lowered herself a bit more, then a bit more, until she realised too late that there was more of her off the shelf than on it, and the next thing she knew she was landing hard on her bottom on a rack of scalding-hot jam tarts.

'Ow! Ooh! Argh!' panted Lana, hopping down from the table, and brushing off the sticky jam tarts as quickly as she could.

Her heart skipped a beat. Now she was on the ground, she could see there was a large alcove in the kitchen wall, and sitting with their backs to her were what could only be a cook and a kitchen boy. Except they weren't moving. All that noise and they hadn't budged an inch.

'Oh, hello,' said Lana politely. 'I didn't see you there.'

Still neither of them moved.

'I fell down the trapdoor,' tried Lana again, edging forward. 'The one in the supermarket.'

But wait. Now she was closer, Lana could see that they were both asleep. The cook was slumped in a chair, and the kitchen boy was snoozing in front of the fire, although the flames appeared to be motionless.

Summoning all her courage, Lana stepped forward, and gently shook the cook by the shoulder.

'Excuse me? Can you help me?'

But the cook showed no sign of waking, so she did the same to the kitchen boy. Both of them were fast asleep.

Lana gulped nervously. Where *was* she?

Her eye caught the clock on the wall. It had stopped dead.

Suddenly she remembered her father! He was waiting for her at the checkout. Wherever she was, she mustn't stay long because she was already in trouble for loading the trolley with all that sugar . . . But on the other hand, this place was so fascinating she couldn't leave without exploring a little . . .

Lana looked around. The sand in the hourglass on the countertop had stopped mid-pour, and the flames in the oven were frozen stiff, like the petals of a giant flower. Over by the sink, something caught the light, and she took a step closer to investigate. Sure enough, a water drop had fallen from the tap, and was now suspended in mid-air, inches above the plughole.

And, what was that on the floor? She crept closer, and her mouth fell open in astonishment. It was a little brown mouse, lying flat on its back, its eyes clamped shut, and its mouth wide open. It was fast asleep!

It was all so strange!

Was she dreaming?

She tiptoed forward into a passageway that led out of the kitchen. The walls were lit by torches, but just like the fire in the oven, their flames were perfectly still. Someone – or something – was sitting on the floor, and as Lana edged closer, she discovered a tall, thin man, his back propped up against the wall, snoring heartily. Wedged between his legs was an enormous chocolate cake, lighting his face with its fifteen unwavering candles.

Was everyone in this place asleep?

The corridor wound left, then right, then led out into an enormous brightly lit hall. A gargantuan banquet table stretched the entire length of the room, crowded with unmoving guests. Each and every one was out for the count: some with their heads on the table, some leaning on the shoulder of the guest next to them; others curled up on the floor. And there, just in front of the giant castle doors, slumped back to back, were the king and queen, surrounded by an entourage of sleeping courtiers.

Lana had never seen a real king or queen before, and for a moment she too froze as still as a statue. Plucking up her courage, she crept towards them. The queen's throat glittered with jewels and her hair was wet, as if she had been swimming. The king was wearing a golden crown, and in his hand was a loaded wooden crossbow. To Lana's astonishment, a little brown bird fluttered out of nowhere and settled on the tip of the arrow, making her jump. It turned its head and stared at her with a beady brown eye.

It was so strange to see something alive and moving among the stillness that, for a moment, Lana couldn't quite take it in. Then, almost as soon as it had landed, the bird took off across the hall. Deep in the shadows was a door, open just wide enough to show a flight of stone steps spiralling upwards, and the little brown bird began to flutter back and forth in the archway, chirruping loudly.

Was it talking to her?

What could it want?

Cautiously, Lana crossed the hall. Sure enough, as she neared the half-open door, the little brown bird fluttered up the flight of steps and out of sight.

Lana had an uneasy feeling about all of this: the frozen cook and kitchen boy; the uneaten food; the motionless king and queen. This was a very odd place indeed. But what if the bird really was trying to show her something important?

She stepped through the archway. The little brown bird was perched on one of the upper steps. As soon as it saw Lana it took off again, flying further up the tower.

So up the spiral staircase Lana went, round and round. Now and then she glimpsed the little brown bird ahead of her. But every time she got close, it took off again, leading her higher and higher into the tower.

Up and up she climbed, and soon her legs began to tire. Determined not to give up, she plodded on, her feet like lead. Then, finally, just when she felt her lungs were about to burst, she turned a corner to find the little brown bird perched on the handle of a tiny oak door.

The door was open, but there was rusty key in its lock.

Lana took a step closer, and the little brown bird fluttered through the doorway.

What could be inside?

Breathing heavily from the climb, and with her heart racing, Lana mounted the final step, crawled through the doorway, and found herself in a dusty room, lit by one small skylight.

In the middle of the room was a bed, and the little brown bird hovered above it, as if this was the thing it had been trying to show her.

There, lying on white linen sheets, shrouded in light, was the most beautiful girl Lana had ever seen. She was fast asleep, with one arm stretched out across the bed; on her fingertip was a single drop of blood.

Lana gasped. She recognised the scene immediately.

There was only one person this could be.

Briar Rose!

She *had* pricked her finger! But where was the spindle?

It was only then that Lana noticed a strange noise – a rolling and rattling, repeating over and over.

At the far side of the room, half hidden in the darkness, there was a woman sitting with her back to Lana. In front of her was a wheel, on which she was spinning thread. She was dressed in a black hooded shawl. At her feet was a jumble of silk and in her left hand was a spindle, turning slowly. That was where the noise was coming from!

As Lana watched, the little brown bird fluttered over, and perched on the woman's shoulder.

'Who's there?' The voice was thin and airy, like wind in dry reeds.

All Lana's thoughts and feelings were suddenly drowned by a crashing wave of fear. She felt her heart racing. She moved her lips to answer, but she was so scared that no words came out.

Gradually, the woman turned. Her hair was white, but her skin was smooth like a baby's. Her eyes were closed and her nostrils were twitching, as if she were trying to smell Lana, rather than see her. She reached out and placed something in Lana's hands. The spindle. Then, slowly, the woman opened her eyes.

They were bright red.

Chapter Six

Down and round the stairs Lana ran, taking two, then three, then four at a time. She pelted across the hall, dodging the sleeping party guests, and bolted down the corridor to the kitchen. She sprinted past the cook and the kitchen boy, before leaping onto the table and reaching up for the top shelf of the cupboard. But she wasn't tall enough!

Her eyes wild, she scoured the room, searching for anything that might help her. There! A shelf full of cookery books! Vaulting down, she took the thickest of them and set it down on the tabletop, then another, and another until she had made a stairway to the top cupboard.

Up she sprang, knocking cheeses left, right and centre as she crawled back up the chute, suddenly happy to be back in the cold and the dark. Round and round she crawled, spiralling slowly upwards, until she reached a tight upward bend. Then, like a spider climbing a spout, she braced her hands and feet against the smooth walls, and began to inch her way upwards.

It was exhausting work. She started to

sweat, which made her hands and arms slip and slide on the walls. Soon, the only thing stopping her falling back down were the rubber soles of her shoes. She felt panic rising in her throat; how was she ever going to reach the top? The burning red eyes of the old woman flashed into her mind and Lana remembered the first part of the story — how the thirteenth fairy had ruby-red eyes. She shuddered. Somehow, no matter how exhausted she was, she had to get out. She had to get home. Taking a deep breath, she made one final scramble, determined to reach the top.

Which was when an extraordinary thing happened. With each tiny movement, Lana felt herself becoming lighter and lighter, until she almost seemed to be weightless.

Soon even the gentlest leg-push propelled her upwards, as if she was an astronaut in zero-gravity, and before she knew it, she was rushing headlong up the chute!

Then, just when she felt she was speeding out of control, the tube twisted, and she began to spiral again, slowing gradually, until suddenly her head struck something hard. She gave one final push and she was back in the supermarket, with her head poking out of the sherbet lemons tub, right in the middle of the pick 'n' mix!

'Dad!'

Lana rushed into her father's arms. She was so pleased to see him! There had been no sign of him at the checkout, but she had finally found him waiting on a bench at the exit, surrounded by shopping bags, talking anxiously on his phone.

'There you are!' he exclaimed, hugging her tight. 'I was just calling Mum.'

'Panic over!' he said into the phone. 'She's here! See you in a bit.' He hung up, and his face clouded. 'Lana, where have you been? I thought I'd lost you.'

'I fell into a fairytale!'

'Lana, please, I'm not in the mood for games. You gave me quite a scare, disappearing like that.'

'It's true! There's a trapdoor in the pick 'n' mix. And it leads right to Briar Rose's castle.'

Lana's father shook his head in mock despair. 'Well, full marks for imagination.

But you know better than to run off in a busy supermarket.'

'It wasn't my fault,' protested Lana.

'Lana, that's enough,' said her father firmly. 'I said there would be a Consequence. So that means no story tonight.'

For the rest of the day, Lana was on her best behaviour. She helped put the shopping away, remembered all her pleases and thank-yous at lunchtime, and spent the afternoon tidying her room. She didn't pester Harrison to play with her and she ate all her green beans at supper without being told. At bedtime she cleaned her teeth for two minutes, just like the dentist recommended, and put her dirty clothes into the washing basket.

The reason was, of course, that she was desperate to avoid her Consequence. As scary as her encounter with the thirteenth fairy had been, it had left her burning with curiosity. Did she really go to Briar Rose's castle? The only way to know for sure was to hear more of the story.

'Are you all right?' asked her mother with a tone of concern, upon finding Lana tucked up in bed of her own accord.

'I thought I'd be good,' replied Lana, 'Because I really want to hear more of *Sleeping Beauty*.'

'Lana, you know that we said no to that story tonight because of what happened at Grimm's.'

'Please!' begged Lana. 'I've been so good all day!'

'Hmmm . . .' said her mother, as if she was in two minds.

'I even brushed my hair and left my clothes out for the morning.'

Her mother gave a tiny smile. Lana could tell she was winning her over.

'Pretty please?' Lana pulled a funny face, and her mother couldn't help but chuckle.

'Well, I suppose it can't really hurt,' she said. 'I'll go and get it. But if you do feel scared you must tell me. I don't want you having nightmares.'

Lana closed her eyes. A warm excited feeling bubbled up inside her at the thought of finding out what would happen next to Briar Rose. She heard her mother's footsteps padding down the hall, the sound of a drawer opening, then the same footsteps padding back again.

There was a loud sneeze and Lana opened her eyes to see her mother sitting beside her, holding the big red-leather story book.

'Dust,' explained her mother, her eyes watering. 'Now, where were we?' she asked, leafing through the pages.

'Spindles,' said Lana. 'The king has just destroyed them.'

'Ah, yes,' said her mother. 'Spindles . . .'

And this . . .

Well, this is pretty much what she read to her ...

True to the king's word, after the banquet, every spindle in the kingdom was destroyed. The very act of spinning itself was declared illegal.

And with no spindles for Briar Rose to prick her finger on, the king and queen stopped worrying about the thirteenth fairy's curse, and life went back to normal. The king took up archery again and the queen got back into wild swimming.

So it was that on her fifteenth birthday, while the servants prepared her birthday lunch, and the king and queen were out pursuing their hobbies, Briar Rose decided to explore the palace. After wandering through the gardens, and browsing the books in the library, she spotted a spiral stone staircase that she had never seen before.

Briar Rose climbed up and up, round and round, until she reached a locked door. Sitting in the lock was a rusty old key. She turned it, and found herself in a tiny room in a turret of the castle.

At the far side of the room, sitting with her back to the door was an old woman. She was working away at something, but Briar Rose couldn't quite see what.

'Hello?' said Briar Rose, but the old woman didn't seem to hear her.

'Excuse me?' said Briar Rose, reaching out to touch the old lady's shoulder. The old lady froze, as if in shock. Then slowly she turned, and the princess was alarmed to see that her eyes were ruby red.

'Forgive me,' said the old woman. 'I was so busy in my work I didn't hear you come in.'

'What are you doing?' asked Briar Rose.

'Why, don't you know what this is?' asked the old woman, with a mischievous grin. As she spoke, she held up a pointed stick, wound with thread.

Briar Rose shook her head.

'It's a spindle, my dear. Watch.'

Briar Rose watched, spellbound, as the old woman unravelled the cocoon of a silk worm, spinning it into thread with the spindle.

The thread shimmered in the light, and looked so beautiful, that Briar Rose wanted nothing more than to press it to her cheek.

'Here, child, come, sit beside me and spin,' the old woman said.

Briar Rose sat and the old woman handed her the spindle. But the instant Briar Rose took hold if it, she pricked herself.

'Oh,' said Briar Rose, as a single drop of blood appeared on the end of her finger. And she slumped off the chair, onto the floor, falling into a deep sleep.

At that very moment, the king and queen stepped inside the front door of the castle, and they also fell into a deep sleep, right there in the hallway. The pages and footmen fell asleep. The cook fell asleep and the kitchen boy did too. The mice in the kitchen fell asleep, the servants fell asleep and so did all the guests that had just arrived for the banquet.

Just as the twelfth fairy had promised, a giant hedge of thorns immediately sprouted around the entire palace, growing tall and thick to protect everyone inside. Soon the hedge was so high that the palace was hidden entirely from view, even its highest turret, where Briar Rose lay sleeping.

'I saw her,' blurted Lana.
'Saw who, darling?'

'Briar Rose. Today, in the supermarket.'

'Oh, how exciting,' said her mother, playing along. 'Was she with Rumpelstiltskin?'

'Mum, I'm not joking. I was in the story! There's a trapdoor,' said Lana, unable to stop herself. 'In the pick 'n' mix. That little old man pushed me into it, and I ended up in the palace. And everyone was asleep! That's where I was when Dad thought I had gone missing.'

'Right,' said her mother decisively, and closed the book. 'I think that's enough of that.'

'But you haven't finished the chapter.'

'No, and I'm not going to. I knew these stories were too scary.'

'But it's true!'

'That's enough, Lana,' said her mother firmly, and turned out the light. 'This book is going away for good.'

Chapter Seven

Having the book of fairytales taken away was very upsetting. The following morning at breakfast, Lana hardly said a word. It had taken her ages to go to sleep, as she couldn't stop thinking about Briar Rose. The thirteenth fairy had tricked Briar Rose once, but what if she did it again? What if she found a way to stop the princess waking up, even after one hundred years? Lana had to go back to the castle — she had to help Briar Rose and make sure the curse was broken.

'Cheer up,' said her father, as he tucked into his apricot jam on toast. 'It's pocket-money day! That usually puts a smile on your face.'

Harrison's ears pricked up. He lowered his book on Archimedes and looked around the table as if he was seeing everyone for the first time.

'Pocket-money day?' he echoed.

'I know, Harrison. Why don't we go to the new supermarket?' Lana suggested, trying not to give anything away in her voice. 'There are so many fun things there.'

'Like what?' asked Harrison.

'Sweets,' said Lana. 'More sweets than you have ever seen in your life. You'll love it.'

'The supermarket again?' asked their mother, wiping her feet on the mat at the back door. She had just been to feed the chickens. She glanced at Lana. 'I thought you said supermarkets were boring?'

'Mostly they are,' said Lana. 'But Grimm's . . . Grimm's is different. Besides, Harrison and I need to spend our pocket money!'

'Okay. If Harrison goes too, you can both walk there. It's not far and the fresh air will do you good,' said her mother with a smile.

Lana felt her heart leap. No parents meant the perfect opportunity to tell Harrison about her plan.

It was still quite early, and Lana and Harrison arrived to find the store with all the lights on, but completely empty, with the doors locked.

'Hmm,' said Harrison, looking at his watch and squinting at the signs on the door. 'It looks like, they don't open for another nine minutes.'

'Harrison . . .' said Lana. 'Have you ever seen a fairy?'

'No,' said Harrison firmly. 'Because there's no such thing.'

'Yes, there is,' said Lana. 'There's one in there. I saw her.'

'There's a fairy in the supermarket?' snorted Harrison.

'Well, not exactly, but there's a trapdoor,' Lana explained. 'In the pick 'n' mix. I slid

down a chute from the sherbet lemons tub and landed in a castle, Briar Rose's castle to be precise.'

'Whose castle?'

'Briar Rose. She's from a fairytale called *Sleeping Beauty*.'

'Lana,' said Harrison, with the air of someone with a lot on their mind, none of which involved trapdoors to fairytales, 'do you think you might possibly have made that up?'

'It's true! If you don't believe me, come and look.'

Suddenly the doors rattled, and they turned to see the little old man on the other side, wrestling with a large bunch of keys. He was dressed as a security guard this time, with a curly mop of ginger hair and a large bushy beard.

'That's the man who pushed me down the chute!' Lana hissed to Harrison. 'He seems to be the only person who works here.'

Finally, the little old man found the right key, and the doors slid open.

'Can I help you?' he asked.

'Probably not,' said Harrison. 'My sister says there's a trapdoor in the pick 'n' mix.'

'No, I didn't!' said Lana, furious that Harrison had just given away what was quite obviously a secret.

'Yes, you did. You said it leads to Briar Rose's castle.'

The little old man began to laugh uncontrollably.

'A trapdoor!' he hooted. 'That's a good one! What a fabulous imagination you have, little girl.' He leant forward slightly and looked Lana right in the eyes. 'What do you know about Briar Rose, anyway? I hope you haven't been reading *Sleeping Beauty*. Because that is clearly much too *scary* a story for you.'

'It's not!' objected Lana, who was getting more than a little fed up of being told what was too scary for her.

'How can a fairytale be scary?' asked Harrison. 'They're just full of princesses and balls and happy-ever-afters. Boring!'

'Trust me,' said the little old man, ominously. 'Fairytales are anything but boring.'

'Anyway,' said Harrison, slightly unsettled. 'I told her you didn't have one.'

'One what?' asked the little old man asked.

'A trapdoor to a fairytale world in your

pick 'n' mix,' replied Harrison.

'Oh, of course not!' scoffed the little man. 'Goodness, the very idea! As I say, what an imagination your sister has! But we do have many of the popular football kits, if that's of interest?' Then he looked around, as if to check no one was watching, and ushered them inside.

Once again, he allowed himself a tiny smile.

Chapter Eight

Harrison brushed past Lana and headed into the store.

'Wait! Where are you going?' she asked her brother. 'The pick 'n' mix is this way.'

'I'm going to check out the football kit. I don't have time for your silly stories.'

'It's true, Harrison! I promise!' called Lana.

But Harrison had already turned the corner. Lana, however, wasn't that easily deterred. She made her way straight to the pick 'n' mix, determined to prove that she was telling the truth.

After making sure that no one was watching her, she borrowed a big plastic box of Lego from the toy section, and stood on it to reach the tub of sherbet lemons.

There was the little cluster of yellow sweets, stuck to the bottom of the tub, just as before. But when she pushed against the hard plastic, it was completely solid. The trapdoor had vanished.

What was going on? Was Harrison right? Had she imagined the whole thing?

'Can I help you?' said a familiar voice, so close it made Lana jump. The little old man's ginger wig and beard were gone, and he was once again wearing his maroon boiler suit, with a matching gold-trimmed hat.

'Where's the trapdoor gone?' demanded Lana. 'And why did you tell my brother I was lying?'

'Brother?' repeated the little old man, with an air of bafflement. 'I've never met your brother.'

Lana felt her temper rising. 'Yes, you have,' she said accusingly. 'These disguises don't fool me. You met him two minutes ago, when you were pretending to be a security guard. You know there was a trapdoor, because yesterday you pushed me into it. And don't say you didn't, because you did!'

'Okay, okay,' hissed the little old man, holding his hands up in a gesture of surrender.

'Keep your voice down. I didn't *push* you. It takes a little force to open the portal, that's all.'

'I knew it! I knew I had travelled to the castle! So where has the . . . portal gone?'

'Nowhere. It's still there, it's just closed.'

Lana narrowed her eyes. 'You're not explaining very well.'

'Each of these sweet tubs is a portal. But they aren't always open, and they don't all lead to the same story. To know when they are open, and where they lead, you need this.' As he spoke, he fished the red-leather booklet from his top pocket and held it up.

'What is that?'

'A timetable,' he replied.

'Like for a bus?' asked Lana.

'Exactly. Let me see . . . liquorice allsorts.

Closed now but in—' He checked his pocket watch – 'fifteen minutes, that will lead to the beginning of *Rapunzel*. Perhaps you know it?'

'Rapunzel, Rapunzel, let down your hair!' chanted Lana.

'Precisely,' said the little old man. 'Though that's later in the story. The beginning is about a pregnant woman, who asks her husband to steal some lamb's lettuce from a witch's garden. If you want the "let down your hair" bit, you'll need the fizzy snakes at half past three on Saturday.'

'What about Briar Rose?' asked Lana.

'What about her indeed?'

'How do I get back into her story?'

The little old man grinned, as if he had finally cornered his prey.

'Remind me, where were you last?'

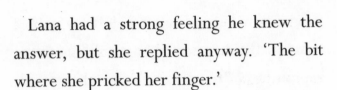

Lana had a strong feeling he knew the answer, but she replied anyway. 'The bit where she pricked her finger.'

'Yes, of course, Briar Rose's fifteenth birthday, I remember. The next stop, I believe, is the arrival of the first prince.' He licked the tips of two long-nailed fingers, and began to flick through the pages of the timetable. '*Sleeping Beauty, Sleeping Beauty, Sleeping Beauty* . . . Ah, you're in luck. There's a portal opening any second.'

'Okay,' said Lana. 'Where is it?'

He pointed with the timetable, directing Lana's gaze. 'Have you tried the dolly mixtures? I hear they are particularly good today.'

By the time Lana looked back, he was gone. Cautiously, she lifted the lid to the dolly

mixtures. The tub was half full. A waft of delicious scent tickled her nostrils, and her mouth began to water. Seizing the trowel, she started to dig, searching for a trapdoor. But every time she took a shovelful of sweets, the rest collapsed to fill the hole. So, rolling up her sleeve, she buried her right arm as far as it would go, stretching out her hand, until the tips of her fingers met the smooth plastic at the bottom of the tub. She gave it an experimental jab, but it didn't budge.

What was it the little old man had said? *'It takes a little force to open the portal.'*

Spreading both hands, she pushed as hard as she could on the top layer of sweets. Again, nothing happened. Somehow, she was going to have to force her way through. So, checking the aisle was empty, Lana hoisted herself up, and launched herself into the tub.

She was hoping that she would go sailing through the portal, but what actually happened was that, for an awkward moment, Lana found herself pinned by her own bodyweight, face-down in a tub full of dolly mixtures with her legs sticking out in the air.

Then suddenly everything gave way and she was hurtling downwards!

Round and down and round and down she raced, until once again the chute swerved sharply downwards, buffeting her so hard it was almost impossible to catch her breath. Just when she felt her lungs were about to burst, it began to spiral, turning in tighter and tighter curls, slowing her almost to a halt, before yawning her out through the hollow of a giant oak tree onto a bed of thick green moss.

Lana took in her surroundings as she lay on the moss, breathing heavily. This time it was night and the air smelled sweet and damp. Above her a full moon shone, illuminating the leafy canopy. Then, sensing something, she held her breath . . .

She could hear voices.

Chapter Nine

Carefully and quietly, Lana pushed herself to her feet. Off beyond the furthest trees a light was flickering. Taking a deep breath, she crept towards it. A young man in a white fur cape was standing by a campfire in a clearing. Beyond him, towering like a cliff face, was a giant wall of thorns.

He must be a prince! Surely he would help rescue Briar Rose? This must be the next part of the story . . .

Lana suddenly realised that it didn't matter that her mother had taken away the book. Not when she could come through the pick 'n' mix portal and visit any fairytale she liked!

Imagine all the exciting adventures she was going to have!

Delighted, Lana crept closer. She could see now that the prince was accompanied by two elderly courtiers, one with a long nose, and one with big ears. They were discussing what might be behind the wall of thorns.

'I have heard,' the long-nosed courtier was saying, 'that beyond is a castle, and in that castle lives a dragon who breathes real fire.'

Lana frowned. That wasn't true at all!

'Why has no one ever seen it, then?' asked the prince.

'He only flies at night,' replied the long-nosed courtier wisely.

'It's night now,' countered the prince.

'The *dead* of night,' said the long-nosed courtier, correcting himself. 'And, anyway, there's a full moon. Dragons never fly on a full moon.'

'Nonsense,' interrupted the big-eared courtier. 'There's a castle, true enough, but no dragon. An ogre lives there, with his eight wives.'

'Eight wives?' asked the prince.

'And twenty-seven baby ogres,' added the big-eared courtier.

Lana frowned again. That wasn't true either. Didn't they know Briar Rose was in there?

'That's a great many ogres,' mused the prince. 'What do they all eat?'

'Sheep,' said the big-eared courtier, without a moment's hesitation.

Lana shook her head. If she didn't do something, Briar Rose might never get rescued.

'You're both wrong,' she said in a loud, clear voice, stepping out of the shadows.

'Who goes there?!' called the big-eared courtier, as he and several others scrambled to their feet.

'Lana.'

'And what manner of creature are you, Lana? A flower-fairy? A shape-shifter?'

'Well . . . I'm a girl.'

'A *girl*?' echoed the prince, as if he had never heard the word before in his life. 'And how, pray tell, do you know what's inside the wall of thorns?'

'I've been in there,' said Lana.

'Really? By what means?'

This didn't feel like the moment to say, 'Through the pick 'n' mix section of my local supermarket', so instead Lana crossed her fingers behind her back and said in a loud, clear voice, 'Magic.'

The courtiers looked at one another.

'Well, do tell us what's inside?' said the prince, smirking at his courtiers, clearly not believing at all that a small girl like Lana could possibly know more than him.

'It's true that there's a castle,' said Lana, stepping forward. 'But there's no dragon, and there's no ogre. There's a sleeping princess. In fact the castle is full of sleeping people.'

'What's the name of the princess?' probed the prince.

'Briar Rose,' replied Lana. 'She pricked her finger on her fifteenth birthday and fell into a deep sleep for a hundred years because of an angry fairy's curse. But there must be a way to rescue her, and her family.'

The big-eared courtier gave a sarcastic laugh. 'Sounds like a very tall tale to me, sire,' he said, smugly.

'On the contrary,' said the prince. 'A curse explains the thorns. Presumably another, kinder fairy put them there as protection?'

'Yes,' said Lana.

'Yes, *sire*,' corrected the long-nosed courtier.

'And this princess . . .' said the prince, looking right into Lana's eyes. 'What's she like?'

'Kind and clever and courageous,' said Lana. 'And lots of other wonderful things. Every one of the twelve fairies gave her a gift—'

'Woah woah woah woah,' said the prince. '*The* twelve fairies? Her family invited *the* twelve fairies, and they came? Fairies only eat from gold plates, so these parents must be very wealthy?'

'I don't know.' Lana shrugged. 'He's a king, so—'

'Trust me,' interrupted the prince, leaning in so that only Lana could hear. 'That means nothing. I'm heir to the throne of Dreitsmark and I'm penniless.' He turned away from her. 'Sir Ulrich!'

The big-eared courtier stepped forward.

'Message the first fairy and ask if she has heard of a princess called Briar Rose.'

The big-eared courtier took a quill, inscribed a short note, fastened it to the leg of a carrier pigeon, then threw the bird high into the air. The startled pigeon circled their heads once, twice, then took off over the forest.

There was a long awkward moment while they all waited for the reply. Lana felt an uneasiness creep over her. The prince seemed interested in Briar Rose because of her money, rather than because she was a good person. That couldn't be right, surely?

'Takes a while,' said the prince to Lana. 'The bird has to fly there, catch the attention of the first fairy, then she needs to reply . . .'

They waited some more.

'Would you like a drink?' offered the prince.

'No, thank you,' said Lana.

The prince made an elaborate performance of scanning the sky. 'It's usually quicker than this.'

Suddenly, there was a flutter of feathers, and the pigeon landed on the big-eared courtier's wrist. The man unravelled a small note and paused for effect, his face unreadable. Then in a loud clear voice he declared, 'The first fairy has indeed heard of Briar Rose. She was a guest at her birth ceremony and gave her the gift of beauty!'

'Then it is true!' exclaimed the prince. 'There is a cursed princess in there who needs rescuing by a gallant prince, who would no doubt be rightfully rewarded by the king and queen!'

Lana tried to smile, but she was having serious doubts about this prince and his reasons for wanting to rescue Briar Rose.

'Sire,' counselled the long-nosed courtier. 'I wouldn't be too hasty . . .'

'Silence!' said the prince, taking off his jacket. 'I'm going in. Sir Ulrich, hand me my sword.'

'B-b-but, sire,' stuttered the big-eared courtier, handing over a delicate-looking sword with a silver jewel-encrusted handle. 'You'll wake the ogres!'

But the prince was already marching towards the wall of thorns.

'Or the dragon!' added the long-nosed courtier.

'Nonsense!' bellowed the prince, as he hacked away at the nearest briar with his weedy sword. 'There's only one thing I'm going to wake, and that's this rich and beautiful princess!' He was making a real mess of slicing through the briar, but eventually, after a lot of huffing and puffing, he just about managed to saw his way through. The severed stump recoiled and a wave of rustling leaves rippled out across the entire wall of thorns, as if a brick had been thrown in the middle of a still pond. Then an extraordinary thing happened. Giant trunks began to twist and turn, and a long tunnel opened up, leading right to the door of the castle.

'Oh,' said the prince, with an air of disappointment. 'I thought it was going to be harder than that.'

'I've got a bad feeling about this,' said Lana.

'Please, your highness,' pleaded the long-nosed courtier. 'I don't think this is wise.'

'Are you sure it's safe, sire?' asked the big-eared courtier.

'I'm about to become stinking rich!' called the prince over his shoulder, as he entered the tunnel. 'What could possibly go—'

Suddenly, the wall of thorns rushed towards him.

'WRONG!'

Chapter Ten

No sooner had the thorns closed in on the prince, than the two courtiers turned to look at Lana.

'It's her fault!' spluttered the long-nosed courtier. 'She's the one that told him about the princess!'

'Seize her!' bellowed the big-eared courtier.

This wasn't what Lana had planned at all!

The poor prince. Lana hoped he was just trapped and nothing worse.

She had to get back to the safety of the supermarket!

Lana started to run. She dodged the big-eared courtier with a swift change of direction, then the long-nosed courtier, by ducking between his legs.

Soon she was among the trees, leaping brambles and crashing through bushes, desperately searching for the hollow tree.

'Let's split up!' she heard the long-nosed courtier cry. 'She's in here somewhere!'

Lana searched high and low, but the hollow tree was nowhere to be seen.

Her heart raced. What would the men do if they found her?

'Would Lana, sister of Harrison, please

make her way to the customer service desk immediately?'

It was the little old man's voice! He was calling her on the supermarket tannoy!

Lana turned on the spot. The sound seemed to be coming from the other side of a large holly bush.

But when she rounded the bush, she saw the long-nosed courtier peering up into the hollow tree. The big-eared courtier joined him, and she stepped back out of sight.

'She's vanished,' said the big-eared courtier, sounding somewhat out of breath.

'*Sssh!*' hissed the long-nosed courtier. 'Didn't you hear the voice before? It was coming from in here.'

The big-eared courtier shrugged. 'I didn't hear anything.'

Lana's mind whirred. Somehow, she had to get past them and into the tree. But how?

Which was when she had an idea. On the ground beside her was a long stick, long enough to reach right through the holly bush. As quietly as she could, Lana threaded it through the centre branches, so that the end was resting against a sprig of holly on the opposite side. Then she started to jostle it to attract the two courtiers' attention.

'Over there!' hissed the long-nosed courtier. 'The bush!'

The big-eared courtier turned to look, before gesturing to his friend that they should go and investigate. Then, silently, they both started to creep towards the dancing sprig.

It had worked! As the men crept behind

the bush one way, she crept round it the other way.

'Sssh!' whispered the long-nosed courtier, drawing his sword. 'I think we've got her.' The big-eared courtier grinned and drew his sword too.

With a loud cry, they leapt forward, stabbing at the sprig of holly, and Lana took off towards the tree!

She was almost there when she heard a shout behind her.

'She's getting away!'

But Lana didn't stop to look back. She ducked into the hollow tree and quickly scrambled up inside. For the first few handholds, all she could feel was spongey rotten wood, then, there it was, the smooth plastic of the chute.

'Grab her feet!'

Her fear at being caught gave her a sudden jolt of energy and she clambered upwards, round and round the twists and turns of the chute. Unlike last time, she didn't even stop to catch her breath, she just wanted to be out and safe.

Before long, the chute straightened out, and Lana found that she was able to stand up inside it. She bent her knees and leapt as high as she could!

For the briefest of moments, she found herself suspended in mid-air. Then ever-so-slowly, a mysterious force began to pull her upwards . . .

Little by little, she began to pick up speed, until she was racing headlong down the tube, before the now-familiar spiralling started, slowing her down and . . . *bump*, her forehead hit something solid, and light streamed into the chute. She pushed up one last time and found herself back in the supermarket, with her head sticking out of a large tub of dolly mixtures.

Chapter Eleven

'Harrison!' cried Lana as she ran towards her brother.

'Ah, here she is!' exclaimed the little old man, who was seated high up behind the customer service desk, talking into a microphone on a bendy silver stalk. His voice boomed out across the store, and he sheepishly flicked a switch.

'Lana!' said Harrison, with a mixture of annoyance and relief. 'Where have you been? I've been really worried. I was going to phone Mum and Dad.'

'I found the trapdoor,' she told him.

'What?'

'In the pick 'n' mix. The portal to the fairytale.'

'Not that again,' said Harrison. 'Where were you really?'

'It's true,' protested Lana, trying to catch her breath. 'I went back into Briar Rose's story. Only a terrible thing happened. I told a prince about Briar Rose, because I wanted him to rescue her. But he got squished by the thorns!'

'Squished?' repeated Harrison.

'Sounds about right,' said the little old

man. 'Worse things than that happen in *real* fairytales, I can tell you.'

'That's enough, Lana,' said Harrison wearily. 'I was trying to be nice by coming here with you, but if you're not going to tell me the truth, then let's just go home.'

'I *am* telling the truth!' said Lana with frustration. 'I promise I am!'

But Harrison just rolled his eyes. 'Don't get me wrong,' he said, putting his hand on her shoulder in a way that made her feel about four years old. 'It's great that you're making your own games up now. But tubs of sweets that lead to fairytales . . . it's just too far-fetched.'

'Harrison!' said Lana, barely able to contain her temper. 'I'm not making this up! When did you become so boring that you can't believe anything that's not in one of your stuffy school books?'

'Might I offer an opinion?' said the little old man, in a voice so calm and reasonable that Harrison and Lana had no choice but to stop arguing and pay attention.

'Working in Customer Services as I do, I am well acquainted with the expectations of those that shop here. And I doubt your brother is going to believe a word of this until he sees it for himself. Now, earlier on, one of my colleagues in Stock Logistics – that's shelf-stacking to you and me – left behind this handy booklet. Handsome-looking chap, I must say. Roughly my height and build. Something about him. Charisma.' As he spoke, he fished the little red-leather timetable from a drawer behind the desk.

'So, might I suggest that you –' he consulted the pages – 'try the jelly tots,' he said, his voice booming out across the store.

For a few moments the little old man stared at the button on the microphone in front of him. He turned it off, then on, then off again.

'I really must get that fixed,' he said.

'Lana,' said Harrison in his Most Serious Voice. 'I am not climbing into a tub full of jelly tots.'

'It's not full,' said Lana. 'It's half empty. Come on, where's your sense of adventure?'

'I haven't got time for games,' he sighed. 'I'm too old for your silliness. I shouldn't even be here now; I should be learning my piano scales. And once I've learned my scales, I need to practise my irregular French verbs. And once I've done that—'

'Harrison!' interrupted Lana. 'You're not listening to me. This isn't a game. Briar Rose is asleep in that palace, surrounded by a wall of thorns. And I really want to make sure that she's rescued, maybe even help if I can . . .'

'Lana,' said Harrison, giving her a pitiful smile. 'It's not happening. Sorry.'

'*Come on*,' said Lana. 'Remember all the times I went along with whatever game you wanted to play, even if I didn't think I'd like it, because I knew you would make anything fun. Now I need you to trust me, just this once. Please.' She linked her fingers to make a cradle.

Harrison slowly shook his head, as if he was doing something he knew he would regret. Then he raised his right foot and rested it on Lana's cupped hands.

'Good decision,' said Lana. 'See you on the other side.'

And with that she launched him head first into the tub.

'Ooof!' Harrison sounded echoey and close up at the same time, as if he had his head in a bucket, which he did. Lana looked up and down the aisle. If someone came looking for pick 'n' mix now, while Harrison's bottom and legs were poking out, they probably wouldn't choose jelly tots.

'Lana! Get me out!' Harrison shouted in a muffled voice, sounding pretty unimpressed.

'Will do!' she said, giving the soles of his feet a very firm push.

'Aaargghhh!'

As soon as he was gone, Lana felt a twinge of anxiety. What if she was leading her brother straight into danger? There were, after all, two sword-wielding courtiers and an evil fairy still on the loose . . .

But it was too late now. After the briefest of glances to make sure no one was watching, she launched herself after her brother.

Chapter Twelve

'Lana?'

'Harrison! Are you okay?'

They were lying on the same bed of moss that Lana had landed in on her last trip. Except now it was early morning, and a fine mist hung above the bracken.

Somewhere deep in the forest, a horn sounded.

'Where are we?' asked Harrison.

'In the fairytale,' said Lana. 'I told you I was telling the truth.'

'What?' Harrison's nose wrinkled in disbelief. 'We can't be . . . can we?'

But before Lana could answer that yes, they could, an enormous white stag came bounding through the trees, heading straight towards them. Without thinking twice, she threw herself on top of Harrison, pushing him to the ground. And just in time, because the creature thundered up the mossy bank, leapt over them, and tore off into the forest.

'You see?' said Lana.

'So?' said Harrison doubtfully. 'A big white deer jumped over us. Doesn't mean we're in a fairytale.'

Suddenly something of terrifying speed

and power split the bark of the oak tree, just above their heads. *Zswing!* Lana realised to her horror that it was an arrow.

'Duck!' she yelled.

Just as she spoke, a second arrow struck, even closer than the first!

Zswing! Zswing!

There were arrows everywhere!

Zswing!

A fourth arrow buried itself in the tree, closer still.

'Stop!' yelled Lana. 'Don't shoot! We're just two kids!'

'Halt!' called a commanding voice. There was the sound of neighing, as hooves churned the ground. 'Who goes there?'

The children looked up. There, looming in the mist, sitting astride a chestnut stallion, was a tall handsome man dressed in hunting leathers and wearing a crown. He must be another prince! As he struggled to control his horse, two knights in armour rode up on either side of him. One had big ears, the other a long nose.

For a horrible moment, Lana thought they might be the two courtiers that had chased her. But they seemed not to recognise her. In fact, now that she looked carefully, she saw they were much younger. Relatives, perhaps?

'Show yourselves,' ordered the prince. 'Stand up!'

Harrison and Lana did as they were told, holding up their hands in surrender.

'Now do you believe me?' whispered Lana to Harrison.

'So?' he whispered. 'They're wearing fancy

dress. That doesn't make it a fairytale either.'

'What brings two children to this forest?' asked the prince.

'Briar Rose,' replied Lana, hesitantly. After all, the last time she had told a prince about the sleeping princess, things hadn't ended that well.

The prince looked perplexed.

'The princess who lives in that castle,' explained Lana, pointing towards the clearing. 'She's asleep behind a wall of thorns. But be careful. The last prince that tried to rescue her got squished.'

She saw a of flash of interest in the prince's eyes.

'Did he indeed? And you know this how?'

'I was here. I saw it. But really I think the only reason the prince wanted to rescue the princess was because her family is rich.'

The prince smiled to himself, as if he knew more than he was letting on.

'I see. And what might your name be, child?'

'Lana. And this is my brother, Harrison.'

'Strange names parents call their children nowadays! I should like to see this wall of thorns, *Lana*, if you would be so kind?'

Together, Lana and Harrison led the prince and his men out from among the trees.

It truly was an impressive sight. A colossal circular wall of thorns, reaching as high as the eye could see. If anything, the briars looked even taller, their trunks thicker, and their thorns even sharper than they had on Lana's earlier visit.

'Now do you believe me?' whispered

Lana to Harrison.

'Fine,' said Harrison casually, trying not to make a big a thing of it. 'So, maybe we actually *are* in a fairytale.'

'Finally,' the prince announced to his men. 'Our quest is at an end.'

'What quest?' asked Lana.

'To free the princess. We've been trying to find this castle for days. But every time we rode into the forest, we got lost. Then today, when we stopped searching, and chased that white stag, it led us straight to you. And you –' he looked at Lana and she felt as if his eyes could see right through her – 'you led us here.'

Lana's eyes widened in alarm. 'No, wait,' she spluttered. 'I told you, the last prince who went into the thorns got squished!'

'I know,' said the prince. 'He was my great-uncle. He came here with two courtiers.'

'One of whom was my great-uncle,' said the knight with the big ears.

'And the other of whom was mine,' added the knight with the long nose.

'But it happened twenty years ago,' said the prince. 'So how could you possibly have been there? After all, you're just a girl.'

'She's telling the truth,' said Harrison, stepping up beside his sister. 'Look, I know this is strange, but . . . we're from another world.'

'Another world?' echoed the prince.

'A supermarket,' said Lana.

'It doesn't really matter,' Harrison said, seeing the confusion in the prince's eyes. 'But everything Lana has told you is true.'

There was a long moment as the prince

considered their words.

'Then I'm grateful to you, Lana of Azupermarket. Your warnings come in good faith. But I must ignore them.' He handed his horse's tether to the big-eared knight. 'Because while we all stand around talking, there's a princess in that castle that needs my help.'

'But——' began Lana.

'My sword, please, Sir Tannhauser.'

'Are you sure about this, sire?' asked the long-nosed knight, as the prince examined the blade of a well-worn battle sword.

'Your great-uncle perished in those thorns,' added the big-eared knight.

'Don't do this!' pleaded Lana.

But it was no use. With one strike, the prince slashed clean through the trunk of the nearest briar and Lana watched as once again the wall of thorns shuddered, revealing a tunnel leading right to the door of the castle. Except this time, as the green fronds retreated, they left behind more than a dozen skeletons.

And before Lana could stop him, the prince stepped boldly into the tunnel.

Chapter Thirteen

Lana covered her face with her hands, not wanting to see the prince get squished in the thorns like his great-uncle. But then she heard Harrison let out a gasp of surprise as the two knights began to laugh and clap.

She lowered her hands . . . The thorns were now covered in beautiful red roses!

'Well?' called the prince, from the tunnel. 'What are you all waiting for? Let's go and find this princess.'

Lana watched as the knights strode through the tunnel of flowers, safely to the door of the castle.

She looked at Harrison, who shrugged his shoulders. It certainly *seemed* safe. They stepped forward together and entered the tunnel. Lana gazed in awe as crimson-red blooms the size of cabbages filled the air with delicious scent.

A scent that reminded her of nothing more than her mother's perfume, *Enchantment*.

A small hatchway was set into the vast wooden gate to the castle. The prince bowed his head and led them all inside.

'Well?' called the prince, from the tunnel. 'What are you all waiting for?
Let's go and find this princess.'

For a moment all five of them stood silently in the shadows of the enormous hall.

Immediately in front of them was a group of sleeping figures. Lana led the prince to the king, still holding his crossbow, and the queen, her hair glistening wet.

'They are Briar Rose's parents,' whispered Lana. 'Everyone in the whole palace is fast asleep.'

'Where is the princess?' asked the prince.

'I'll show you,' said Lana.

The last time she had climbed the tower, Lana had almost keeled over with exhaustion, but she was now so excited to rescue Briar Rose that she practically skipped to the top. It was only when they arrived, and she saw that the little oak door was still ajar, that a terrifying thought struck her: what if the evil thirteenth fairy was still there?

But she swallowed her fear and went inside anyway. Much to her relief, there was no sign of the fairy or the spindle. Instead, lying on the bed with one arm outstretched was the princess.

'My lady?' enquired the prince, in his most princely voice. But the sleeping Briar Rose didn't stir.

'Wake up, my lady,' he said, approaching the princess.

Nothing.

'My lady?' he bellowed. But Briar Rose showed no sign of waking.

'Hmm,' said the prince, mulling it over. His eyes lit up, as a thought struck him. 'Perhaps she's ticklish.' He plucked the feather from his hunting cap and brushed it gently over the crook of Briar Rose's elbow. But Briar Rose didn't move a muscle.

'Giddy-widdy,' he goaded, tickling under her chin. 'Rise and shine!' But Briar Rose remained out for the count.

Defeated, the prince put the feather

back in his cap.

'It's no use. She's fast asleep.'

'What about kissing her on the cheek?' Lana said. 'That's how my Mum and Dad wake me up.'

'Kissing her,' repeated the prince, thinking it over. 'No, I don't think that's right. Not without asking first. And I can't ask because she's asleep . . . Unless, maybe I could try a polite kiss on her hand?'

Lana and Harrison said they thought that was an acceptable idea.

So, leaning over, the prince planted a kiss on the back of Briar Rose's outstretched hand. No sooner had he done so, than her eyelids began to flutter, and she opened her eyes.

'Do excuse me,' said the prince, hurriedly, as Briar Rose sat up in confusion. 'My name is

Otto von Duresberg, first in line to the throne of Dreitsmark. I have come to rescue you.'

Lana cleared her throat and stared at the prince pointedly, who quickly added, 'With my companions, Lana and Harrison of Azupermarket.' He gestured towards Lana and Harrison who waved awkwardly.

'Did someone kiss me?' asked Briar Rose, slightly put out.

'Yes, sorry about that,' said the prince, with a nervous laugh. 'That was me. Just on your hand, though, but we were running out of ideas for how to wake you.'

'You've been asleep,' explained Lana.

'For a really long time,' added Harrison.

'Wait,' said Briar Rose, suddenly remembering. 'There was an old woman . . . She was spinning and I . . .' Her voice trailed away, as she saw the drop of blood on her finger.

'That was no ordinary old woman,' confided Lana. 'That was the thirteenth fairy. The one who put the spell on you.'

Briar Rose looked at her blankly.

'Didn't your parents tell you about the thirteenth fairy?'

Briar Rose shook her head.

Lana took a deep breath and explained the story as she knew it.

'If a fairy cast a spell on me when I was a baby, why didn't anyone tell me?' asked Briar Rose in disbelief.

'Maybe they didn't want to scare you,' suggested Lana.

'I need to speak with my parents.'

Briar Rose moved to stand up, but she

was still weak from her long sleep and as quickly as she rose she had to sit straight back down again.

'Prince Otto,' smiled Briar Rose. 'I don't suppose you'd be kind enough to help me down the stairs?'

When they arrived in the hall, instead of a roomful of silent statues, there was nothing but noise and confusion. Everyone had come back to life, without the slightest idea they'd been asleep.

'Well?' bellowed the king. 'Where is she?'

'Not in the library, sire!' called a courtier.

'Not in the kitchen, either!' called another.

'Get back! Get back!' cried the queen, as the tall, thin butler arrived with the lit birthday cake. 'It's meant to be a surprise!'

'Your Majesties,' declared the prince,

bowing deeply.

'Sssh!' hissed the king. 'We're looking for Briar Ro—'

The king fell silent, seeing his daughter had her hand on the prince's arm.

'Your Majesties,' announced the princess, clearly enjoying the look of horror on their faces. 'May I present Prince Otto of Dreitsmark, and his companions Lana and Harrison of Azupermarket?'

'Prince What of Where?' asked the king, floundering.

'Prince Otto of Dreitsmark,' repeated the prince, helping Briar Rose to sit down on a nearby chair. 'You may know my father, King Otto the Sixth?'

'I know a King Otto the *First*,' said the king tetchily.

'Ah, yes,' said the prince. 'He was my great-great-great-great-grandfather.'

The king and queen stared at him.

'You've been asleep,' explained Harrison. 'For a really, really long time.'

'Asleep?' echoed the queen.

'You all have,' said Lana, holding up the spindle. 'The thirteenth fairy's spell came true.'

There was an uneasy murmur from the courtiers and guests.

'What?' asked the king. 'It can't have done. I had every one of those wretched things destroyed. Where did you get that?'

'If you don't believe me,' said Lana, 'then step outside.'

One by one, the king, queen, their courtiers and their guests emerged from the dark musty hall, out into the rose-covered tunnel.

'Look, everyone,' called Lana, as she led them out into the sunshine. 'Look what grew while you were asleep.'

The wall of thorns was now a wall of roses, stretching as high as the eye could see.

'Then it's true,' said the king. He looked at the queen. 'I failed to keep our daughter safe.'

'You did your best,' said the queen gently. 'We both did.'

'Why didn't you tell me?' demanded Briar Rose.

'We didn't want to scare you,' replied the queen.

'But how can I avoid danger if I don't know it's there?'

'Dear child,' said the king, taking Briar Rose's hand. 'You are quite right. I've been a fool. How can I ever earn your forgiveness?'

There was a pause, and Briar Rose softened. 'You can tell me the truth. And you can give me a really fantastic birthday party.'

There was silence for a moment, then the king chuckled. He held out his arms and embraced Briar Rose, and the queen beamed an enormous smile. One by one, the courtiers began to applaud, delighted at seeing the royal family united once again, and more than a little relieved at having woken up after one hundred years fast asleep.

And as the happy group laughed and clapped, the little brown bird that had been perched on the rose arch decided it had seen and heard enough. Chirruping excitedly, it flapped its wings and took off onto the wind.

Chapter Fourteen

Briar Rose's party passed in a blur. Luckily, the curse had kept everything fresh, despite it being one hundred years old. A suckling pig arrived, high on the shoulders of four kitchen porters, and was followed by game pie, roast squash and buttered greens. After that came Lana's old friends, the cheeses from the cheese cupboard, followed by the cream horns, fruit scones and (slightly squashed) jam tarts and, finally, when everyone was fit to burst, out sailed the birthday cake, lit with one hundred and fifteen candles.

No sooner had Briar Rose blown them out, when in sprang a troupe of tumblers, climbing higher and higher on each other's shoulders, climaxing in a human pyramid. Next came a strong man, who lifted eight sacks of flour with a wooden yoke; then, finally, a band of musicians played a merry jig and everyone got up to dance. Lana found herself swept away, like a piece of driftwood, on wave after wave of pure joy.

But it was when she saw the king and queen dancing with Briar Rose that Lana suddenly thought of her own parents. As fun as it was here, she and Harrison needed to get home, before their mum and dad missed them and started to worry. So she pushed her way through the crowd, until she found her brother, dancing in a circle with Prince Otto and the two knights.

The music was now so loud that Lana had to shout directly into his ear.

'I think we need to go back!' she shouted.

'Sorry,' said Harrison.

'I SAID I THINK WE NEED TO GO BACK!'

'I know,' smiled Harrison. 'And I was saying sorry. For not believing you about the portal.'

'Oh,' said Lana. 'That's okay.'

'And I'm sorry for being so serious about everything recently,' said Harrison. 'I've been so worried about school and studying that I forgot that sometimes it's important just to have fun.'

Lana smiled. She had her brother back.

'Can we come here again some time?' asked Harrison.

Lana felt a warm, happy feeling inside. 'Any time you like,' she replied, beaming.

After they had bowed to the king, and curtsied to the queen, and wished Briar Rose one last 'happy birthday', and hugged both her and the prince, and then hugged them again, and then promised to come back very soon, and then hugged them both one more time for luck, Harrison and Lana crept out of the giant castle door, through the tunnel of sweet-smelling red roses, and into the night.

The grass in the meadow was wet with dew, and by the time they reached the woods their shoes and socks were soaked. Luckily, the moon was still high enough to light their way, and they soon found the tree with the hollow in it. The first part of the chute was always the trickiest, so Lana let Harrison climb up ahead of her, in case he got stuck.

'I keep slipping!' squeaked Harrison, from inside the chute.

'Press on the sides,' she shouted, 'and work your way up. The higher you go, the easier it gets.'

'Oh, Lana of Azupermarket?'

Lana ducked back out of the hollow.

Prince Otto was standing in the clearing, half shadowed by the moonlight.

'As soon as you'd gone, I remembered that there is something I want you to have.' He held out a hunting horn. 'Even the wiliest of sprites need help sometimes. If you ever need me, call on this.'

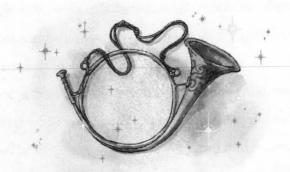

And with that, he melted back into the shadows.

Then he came back for one more hug.

Then he melted back again.

The next thing Lana knew, a trowel was prodding at her forehead. It was Harrison.

'Ow!' she yelped, as she struggled out of the tub. 'What was that for?'

'Sorry. Just I thought it would be nice to get some jelly tots as a souvenir. We've got our pocket money, so we might as well spend it.'

Of course, once they had each collected some jelly tots, it seemed wrong not to add a few dolly mixtures and sherbet lemons, to remind Lana of her previous two visits. And then they added some chocolate drops, refreshers, fizzy snakes, and fried eggs for good measure.

The problem was, of course, that the sweets were so tempting, and the queue at the checkout so long, that by the time they'd reached the till the bags they had filled up were now, well . . . a little bit empty.

'Hmm,' said the little old man, as he put their nearly-empty bags on the weighing scales (he was now, unsurprisingly, back on the till in his waistcoat and pillbox hat). 'Are you sure this is everything?'

Harrison and Lana nodded guiltily.

'One moment, please.' He picked up a telephone from beside the till and dialled. 'Hello, it's Till Four here. Could I speak to security?'

'We might have eaten one or two fizzy snakes while we were in the queue,' offered Harrison.

'I think I had a chocolate drop,' added Lana.

'Okay, I'll find him myself,' said the little old man into the phone. 'Wait here, please,' he said to Harrison and Lana, lifting the barrier to the till, and heading off into the store.

'Sorry,' said Harrison to everyone behind them in the queue.

No sooner had the little old man disappeared from sight, when he reappeared as a security guard, complete with ginger beard and wig.

'I've got eyes on them now,' he said into a walkie-talkie. 'I do apologise for the inconvenience, ladies and gentlemen,' he said to the rest of the queue. 'Normal service will be resumed as soon as demonly – I mean *humanly* – possible.' Then he took hold of Harrison's and Lana's upper arms and frogmarched them into a room at the back of the store and closed the door behind them.

Lana looked around, taking in the small,

dark room. One wall was completely covered in screens that showed different sections of the shop floor. The little old man picked up a remote and pointed to the screen that showed the toy aisle, specifically the pick 'n' mix section.

Suddenly Lana remembered the hunting horn the prince had given her. Now, when the little old man wasn't looking, seemed a good time to hide it.

The little old man pressed rewind on the remote control and the image on the screen whirred backwards in time, until eventually black-and-white versions of Harrison and Lana appeared, clearly filling their bags to the brim with sweets. He pressed pause.

'How old are you, Harrison?'

'Twelve.'

'Twelve,' repeated the little old man.

'That makes you the responsible partner in this little debacle.' He tapped on the pick 'n' mix screen with a bony knuckle. 'This one's, what, eight?'

'Nine,' Lana reminded him.

'Right. Nine, so I think a judge would look favourably. But you –' he pointed to Harrison – 'you should know better.'

'I'm sorry,' said Harrison. 'We both are, aren't we, Lana?'

Lana nodded. 'We won't do it again, we promise,' she said, using her most innocent-looking face.

There was a long pause, as if the little old man was weighing up several extremely attractive options.

'I hope you both enjoyed Briar Rose's party? It's a fun portal that one. Just a shame that things don't really work out that well in that story.' He tutted sadly.

'What do you mean?' Lana said. 'That's the end of the story, isn't it? The happy-ever-after?'

The little old man shook his head and tutted again. 'Oh, the innocence of babes.'

He took a deep breath through his nostrils, and grinned.

'Look, why don't I forget all about the stealing?' he offered. 'And in return, Harrison, you can promise to read your sister the rest of the story when you get home. Find out what happens at the end of *Sleeping Beauty*, eh? Although, I warn you that it's probably much too scary.'

'I can read, you know,' said Lana, annoyed that yet again she was being told that the story was too scary for her. 'And I'm not afraid of a fairytale.'

'I'm sure you *can* read,' smiled the little old man. 'But I want Harrison to hear it too. Because you're a team now, aren't you? Am I right, Harrison?'

Even though he thought the little old man was really weird, Harrison nodded.

'Good boy. Yes, you finish that story, and it'll be like this never happened.' He opened the door, inviting them to leave. 'Well, run along, children, and don't ever let me catch you stealing sweets from this store again.'

As soon as the children had gone, the little old man grinned. He had to hand it to himself: everything was going exactly to plan.

Chapter Fifteen

That night, for the longest time, Lana lay wide awake in the darkness, unable to sleep. It had been a long day and Harrison said he was too tired to read the rest of the story, promising that they'd read it in the morning. She turned over and stared at the hunting horn on her bedside table, thinking about the weird and wonderful events of the past few days. The little old man couldn't have been right, could he? Surely Briar Rose was safe now that the thirteenth fairy's curse was broken?

She closed her eyes, willing herself to go to sleep. Of course everything was fine. The little old man had been mean to her from the moment they met, and now he was just trying to frighten her. Nothing more.

Feeling calmer, Lana closed her eyes and began to drift off, but as she did an image formed in her mind. Briar Rose and Prince Otto were standing under a rose arch in the palace garden. Both of them were older; the sun was shining, Briar Rose wore a beautiful white wedding dress and, as the pair kissed, all the guests leapt to their feet, applauding wildly. The king and queen beamed happily at one another.

But then something strange happened. Briar Rose was trying to speak, but no words were coming out. Her hair began to float, as if she was underwater, and she reached out, her eyes widening in fright, as if she was struggling to breathe. 'Help me, Lana,' she mouthed. 'Help!'

Lana opened her eyes. What did that vision mean? Was Briar Rose in danger?

She had to find out what happened next in the story . . .

Her brother was all twisted up in his bedclothes and snoring softly.

'Harrison,' she whispered, shaking him gently by the shoulder. 'Wake up.'

Harrison opened his eyes, then shut them again.

'I had a really weird dream. I think Briar Rose is in trouble.'

'Go to sleep, Lana.'

'Wake up!' insisted Lana, shaking her brother and accidentally nudging his Soldier Force display, which began to cascade down the shelves beside his bed, making a horrendous racket.

'Lana!' hissed Harrison in irritation, doing his best to stem the flow of plastic soldiers. '*Ssshh!*'

'We need to find the book!'

'It'll be in Mum's sock drawer. It's where she puts everything she doesn't want us to find.'

'Okay,' said Lana, and padded off across the landing.

There was a long pause while Harrison

battled with his thoughts. One part of him wanted nothing more than to go back to sleep and forget about fairytales and Lana. But another, slightly bigger part of him was curious to know what happened to Briar Rose. Besides, if it really was as scary as the little old man said, Lana would need some company.

So, when Lana came quietly out of their parents' room with the book, heading for her bedroom, he hissed for her to join him.

'Put my light on,' he said. Then he opened the book of fairytales, turning the pages until he found the part of the story where Briar Rose and the prince got married, and began to read out loud.

And this . . .

Well, this is pretty much what he read . . .

After some time, Briar Rose and the prince fell in love, and got married. The prince came to love the king and queen as he would his own parents, and they all lived happily together in the castle as one family. The king and the prince spent their afternoons practising archery, while Briar Rose and her mother enjoyed wild swimming together in the newly restored castle moat.

More time passed, and Briar Rose gave birth to twins, a boy and a girl. The king and queen were delighted with the new arrivals to the palace and suggested a grand party, but Briar Rose and the prince politely declined, with thoughts of the thirteenth fairy and Briar Rose's curse in their minds. Instead, they gave their two children the simple names of Hansel and Gretel, and had a small gathering for a few close friends.

As more time passed, Briar Rose and the prince grew tired of the pomp and ceremony of the palace, and decided to step away from their royal duties. They moved out of the castle into a simple house on the edge of the village and sent Hansel and Gretel to the village school. Briar Rose made and designed her own range of swimwear, which was extremely popular, and the prince set up a hunting shop that made premium bows and arrows, much to the joy of the king, who became his best customer.

But their problems were far from over. Unbeknown to them, the thirteenth fairy was now living in a cottage in the middle of an enormous forest. By now her years of wicked spells had made her an outcast with the other fairies, and she had taken on her truer form as a witch. Her magic had become stronger than ever and the little brown bird that had once been her companion had now become her familiar.

A familiar, as you probably know, is an animal that acts as a witch's eyes and ears, and helps her work her magic. One day, as the witch was tending her garden, the bird alighted on a nearby tree and began to sing.

'Tra la la and a tra la lee. She has beauty for all to see!' sang the bird.

'Who does?' enquired the witch, but the little bird flew away without giving her an answer.

The following day, as the witch was sowing lettuce, the little bird reappeared. 'Tra la lee and a tra la la. The prince he came from a country far.'

'What prince?' demanded the witch, but once again the bird just flew away.

On the third day, the witch decided to trick the bird. When it started to sing, she pretended she couldn't hear and just went on tending her garden.

'Tra la loo and a tra la liss. The prince he woke her with a kiss,' sang the bird. But the witch ignored it.

'Tra la lee and a tra la loy, she bore two children, a girl and a boy,' sang the bird, hopping a little closer. Still the witch said nothing.

'Tra la lee and a tra la loon, two children fair as the Sun and Moon,' the bird sang, hopping right onto the handle of the hoe the witch was using.

Quick as lightning, the witch snatched the little bird by its wing. 'Tell me who you are speaking of,' she threatened as it fluttered helplessly, 'or I'll pull your feathers out one by one.'

'Don't hurt me, mistress, please,' begged the little bird. 'I'll tell you everything I know.'

'I'm listening,' said the witch.

'Briar Rose, the princess you put a spell on, has woken up. She's married Prince Otto, the son of King Otto the Sixth of Dreitsmark, and she plans to live happily ever after.'

The witch burst into laughter, as if it was the funniest thing she had ever heard. 'Does she indeed?' she chuckled.

'Please, please, let me go,' begged the bird. 'And I'll never tease you again.'

'Very well,' said the witch. 'But first, I've got a job for you.'

Soon after, the prince's father, King Otto

the Sixth, was admiring himself in his bedroom mirror when the same little bird tapped on the window glass.

'Please, please, come quickly,' it chirped. 'Someone's being robbed in the woods.'

Now, the king was a good man and so wasted no time in coming to the rescue. He arrived in the wood to find robbers trying to steal from a beautiful damsel. So he saw off the thieves, lifted the lady up onto his horse, and carried her back to his castle. There he gave her cool water to drink, and fed her bread and honey from a golden plate.

'At last,' said the damsel with satisfaction. 'A king who knows how to treat a lady.'

Of course the king fell in love with her immediately, and they were married the very next day.

But the damsel was really the witch in disguise, and while the king was greeting the wedding guests, the new queen stole upstairs to his bedchamber. She took up the king's pen and wrote a note, copying his handwriting exactly:

Beloved daughter-in-law,
I should very much like to meet you and my grandchildren and for you all to meet my new bride. Please come and see me at your earliest convenience.
  Yours faithfully,
  King Otto the Sixth of Dreitsmark

The queen stamped the letter with the royal seal, to make sure it appeared the king had written it himself. Then she sent the note to Briar Rose by messenger.

It so happened that when the note arrived the prince was away on a hunting trip but, excited by the invitation, Briar Rose decided to make the journey alone with the children, leaving a letter for her husband so he could join them on his return.

It was a long and difficult journey, and when Briar Rose and the two children arrived at the castle, she was surprised to find it empty of everyone except the new queen.

'Briar Rose,' said the queen warmly, 'thank you so much for coming.'

'Do I know you?' asked Briar Rose, feeling a flicker of recognition.

'We met twice, very briefly,' replied the queen. 'When you were younger. Once at your birth ceremony, and once at one of your birthday parties. I was a friend of your father's. And now I am your mother-in-law.'

Briar Rose frowned slightly. Something didn't seem quite right, but she wasn't sure what . . .

'Where is the king?'

'He has gone to prepare our house in the country, and I am to bring you to him.'

'That sounds wonderful!' said Briar Rose. 'When do we leave?'

'Now,' said the queen.

'Really?' asked Briar Rose in concern. 'But the children and I are very tired from the journey.'

'I'm afraid so,' replied the queen. 'That way we can be there by nightfall.'

And so without delay, the queen and Briar Rose set off along the forest path, with Hansel and Gretel following behind. Eventually, after many hours' riding, they came to a wide river.

'Come,' said the queen. 'The river is very fast, so we must cross by boat.' She helped them in and took the oars. 'See how fast the river runs?' she called, as they reached the middle, where the current ran quickest. 'They say if you look into the water, you can glimpse your future.'

'I can see fire,' said Hansel, looking over-board, and seeing the reflection of the sun.

'I can see earth,' said Gretel, peering into the depths, and glimpsing the bottom of the river.

'All I can see is water,' said Briar Rose, leaning towards the river. And then, quick as a flash, the queen pushed her in!

Of course, Briar Rose was a strong swimmer

with lots of experience in wild water, and though the current was fast, she fought bravely against it.

'Help me,' spluttered Briar Rose. 'I'm drowning!'

'Stupid girl!' taunted the queen. 'It's me, the thirteenth fairy, now the most powerful witch in all the kingdoms.' As she spoke, her hair turned white and her eyes clouded red.

'Help us, Mother!' called Hansel and Gretel.

'Goody-goody Briar Rose can't help you now!' crowed the witch, amidst gales of cruel laughter. 'No one can!'

Chapter Sixteen

Harrison looked up at Lana. Brave Briar Rose was drowning, and poor Hansel and Gretel were in the clutches of the witch!

'I know the story of Hansel and Gretel,' said Lana gravely. 'Mum told me about it.'

'What happens?'

'The witch wants to eat them.'

Harrison nodded slowly. 'And does she?'

'I don't know! But Briar Rose is in danger, and so are Hansel and Gretel.' Lana took a deep breath. 'We have to go back through the portal and save them.'

Without a sound, Lana stole back to her room and began to get dressed, knowing that Harrison was doing the same. Then she picked up the prince's hunting horn and slung it round her neck.

'So, what's our plan?' ventured Harrison, as they stole across the supermarket car park. The air was cold and damp, and up ahead of them, Grimm's was wreathed in mist.

'Simple,' Lana replied, holding up the horn. 'We go back into the story and blow on this. Then the prince will come and save them.'

'Right,' said Harrison, not entirely

convinced. 'What if he doesn't hear it?'

'He'll hear it,' replied Lana confidently. She rattled the glass doors. They were firmly locked.

'But what if he doesn't?'

Suddenly, two giant beams of light sprang from the darkness and swept across the car park. A lorry was approaching.

'Quick!' rasped Lana. 'This way! Let's try the back.'

Crouching low, she raced along the front of the store, and turned the corner. But the back of the store was protected by a high fence, topped with coils of barbed wire.

'Over there!' hissed Harrison. 'Look, a gap.'

Two of the metal fence posts were dented, creating a space that was just wide enough to squeeze through. At least, it was for Lana. When Harrison came to try, however, he found he wouldn't fit. Ahead of them, the lights of a lorry arced across the loading bay.

'What now?' squeaked Lana.

'The lever principle!' exclaimed Harrison, pointing to a pile of rusting ironwork on Lana's side of the fence. 'Pass me that pole!'

'I can't lift that; it's too heavy!'

'Then drag it!'

As quickly as she could, Lana dragged the pole to the gap in the fence, and Harrison pulled it through. On the other side of the bay, the lorry paused by a security gate.

Summoning all his strength, Harrison lifted the pole like a weight lifter, wedged one end into the gap, and pushed. For a few seconds, nothing happened. Then there was a buckling sound, and the gap widened!

'Give me a lever long enough,' whispered

Harrison, as he joined Lana on the other side. 'And I will move the world.'

Lana looked at him in a way that said: I have no idea what you are talking about.

'Archimedes,' explained Harrison.

Now she remembered. He'd been studying Archimedes when he wouldn't come and play. Lana felt a twinge of guilt. Maybe she had been wrong to feel so upset with Harrison for studying so hard . . .

She was about to tell him just that when the lorry revved its engine and trundled through the open security gate into the compound.

With an impossibly loud hiss of its brakes, the lorry jolted to a halt, and a familiar figure vaulted down from the cabin. The little old man threw open the loading-bay doors and switched on the lights. This time he was dressed as a lorry driver, with maroon dungarees, a cap and a purple goatee beard. With the loading-bay doors open he trotted back to the cabin, hauled himself up into the driver's seat and started the engine.

'Come on!' urged Harrison. 'Now's our chance to get inside!'

They began to run as the lorry started reversing with a loud *beep-beep-beep*. Scouting around the vehicle, Harrison and Lana rushed inside, just before the lorry entered.

To begin with, all they could see was a yellow forklift truck and tower after tower of supermarket goods, wrapped in thick plastic and stacked on wooden pallets. They raced behind one of the stacks, just as the lorry hissed to a halt, and the little old man started to climb down from the cabin again.

'A familiar figure vaulted down from the cabin.'

'Over there!' whispered Harrison, spotting a door.

Seconds later, they were on the other side, struggling to catch their breath. They found themselves in a long corridor with purple walls. There were lots of gold doors leading off it. Harrison tried one. A toilet. He tried another. A broom cupboard. Then Lana tried the next. Phew. The shop floor.

They silently ran to the pick 'n' mix section.

'How do we know which tub to go through?' asked Harrison.

'Good point,' said Lana. 'We need a copy of the timetable. Wait here.'

A few moments later, she returned.

'Got it,' she said triumphantly. 'He keeps one at customer service, remember? Right . . . *Sleeping Beauty, Sleeping Beauty, Sleeping Beauty . . .*

"Wedding", no, "The Witch and the Little Bird", no . . . got it! "Briar Rose in the River". let's see, it's Friday . . .'

'Saturday,' corrected Harrison. 'At 3.30 am.'

'Saturday at 3.30 am . . .' repeated Lana. 'So we need to travel through the . . .' She frowned as she scanned the long list of times and sweets. 'Mint imperials!'

And saying that, she threw back the lid of the mint imperials tub, ready for their next adventure!

Chapter Seventeen

Moments later, Lana was racing head first down the chute, pursued by a half a tub's worth of mint imperials, closely followed by Harrison. The ride seemed longer than all the others put together, chasing up, down, right, left, then corkscrewing around and around, before finally plunging them into fast-moving, ice-cold water!

Lana only just had time to catch her breath before she found herself rolling head over heels, water rushing into her ears, with no idea which way was up and which was down. She needed to find the surface, and quickly before she ran out of air! She was starting to panic, but then she saw the sun, shimmering faintly beneath her and, summoning every ounce of strength, lungs bursting, she turned in the water and swam with all her might towards it . . .

Her head broke the surface, and she took in a giant gulp of air.

'Lana! Quick! Hang onto this!' called Harrison. Relieved to hear his voice, she turned just in time to see her brother racing past, his arm outstretched, clinging to a log. Their hands clasped and suddenly she was rocketing through the rapids alongside him.

The river was unimaginably wide, banked on either side by an immense silver birch forest, stretching in every direction as far as the eye could see. A pale sun was shining through the clouds, and a sharp wind was whipping the slate-grey water into white foam peaks.

'Kick your legs! We need to steer to the shore!' called Harrison. Lana did as she was told, and little by little, the log began to turn towards the bank, like an ocean-liner heading for port. Soon their feet were able to touch the bottom of the river, and they hauled themselves up onto the pebble-strewn shore, struggling to catch their breath.

'Thanks,' said Lana. 'If it hadn't been for

you, I might have drowned.'

But Harrison wasn't listening. 'I don't understand,' he said. 'Where's the boat?'

He was right: the river was empty.

'Harrison, look. Smoke!'

It was true. Way off in the distance, where the forest rose to meet the sky, was a tiny plume of blue smoke.

'Uh-oh,' replied Harrison. 'That must be where the witch lives.'

'That means . . .' Lana hesitated, not wanting to say it out loud.

'Briar Rose has drowned, and the witch has got Hansel and Gretel,' finished Harrison.

'Right,' said Lana, reaching for the horn round her neck, grateful it hadn't gotten lost in the rapids. 'I'm going to call the prince!'

With a flourish, she put the horn to her

lips, took a deep breath and blew!

But all that came out was a strange bubbling sound.

'Maybe it's wet?' suggested Harrison.

Lana frowned. She tipped the horn upside down, and sure enough, out trickled a stream of river water.

'Give it a shake.'

Lana did as Harrison suggested, then blew again. Still nothing.

'Let me have a go,' said Harrison. But he couldn't get it to work either. 'It's the bend,' he announced, putting the wide end of the horn to his eye, like a telescope. 'It's full of water.' He handed the horn back to Lana. 'We need it to dry out.'

Lana nodded. 'But how?'

Harrison shrugged. 'I don't know, but we

don't have time to think about that right now. We need to get to the witch's house and save Hansel and Gretel.'

'But how do we get across the river?' The water was as wide as a motorway, and its rapids were racing past like cars in the fast lane.

'Maybe there's a bridge?'

'Maybe,' said Harrison. 'But this place looks pretty deserted.' It was true. There were no signs of human life anywhere, just the reeds rustling at the top of the bank, the giant grey sky, and the immense silent forest.

Then Harrison wiped his wet hair from his face and smiled a broad smile. 'Oxbow lakes.'

'I'm sorry?'

'Remember, I was studying them for geography? We need to go upstream because the further we go, the narrower the river will be. If we go far enough, we'll be able to get across.' Lana nodded. The lever principle, swimming practice, oxbow lakes . . . All the work, study, and training her brother did was definitely coming in handy. 'But we need to hurry if what you said about the witch eating the children in the story is true.'

Lana gulped. She really hoped it wasn't.

As fast as they could, Lana and Harrison began to run along the bank, picking their way among the boulders at the water's edge. Of course, on a normal day, if Lana had fallen into an ice-cold river wearing nothing more than jeans, her favourite unicorn sweatshirt, and pink All-Stars, she'd have needed a hot bath, ten episodes of something, and a change of clothes before she would even slightly calm down. But right now, nothing was further from her mind. All that mattered was getting to that plume of smoke in time to save Hansel and Gretel.

'Wait,' panted Harrison, pulling her to a halt. 'What's that?'

'Where?'

'Up ahead, in the water.'

Lana looked to where he was pointing, but all she could see were waves, whipped up by the wind. Then, suddenly, in the middle of the river, something flashed white.

'A rock?' suggested Lana.

'It's moving.'

He was right. Something was crossing the river. And fast. As it reached the shallows, it reared up on two jet-black legs, raised its wings, arched its neck and began to sprint through the water towards them.

'A swan! And it's charging at us!' cried Harrison. 'RUN!'

They turned on their heels, ready to run back the way they had just come, but then something extraordinary happened. The swan called out to them!

'Lana! Harrison!'

They both halted mid-stride. It's one thing to read about talking animals in a fairytale, but quite another to have one yell at you in broad daylight. Thinking that maybe they hadn't heard, the swan rose to its full height and began to beat its wings on the water, sending arcs of spray high into the air.

'Don't be scared! It's me, Briar Rose!' said the huge swan. Now that it was closer, Lana could see that the bird was taller than a grown-up, with a wingspan to match.

'Hi,' called Lana, slightly freaked out. She was delighted her friend was safe, but she wasn't sure whether or not it was polite to point out she was now a swan, or to ask how that had come about.

'Nice to see you again,' called Harrison, unable to hide the puzzled look on his face.

'You too, but hurry!' hollered the swan, beckoning with the crook of her wing. 'I'll carry you across the river!'

'What if it's a trick?' Harrison said quietly. 'What if it's the witch in disguise?'

But the swan had now come close enough that Lana could see into her eyes. 'It's not the witch,' she said confidently. 'It's Briar Rose.' Then she splashed forward and threw her arms around the swan's neck. Briar Rose closed her eyes and laid her head on top of Lana's. For a moment, they stood there, child and swan together.

'Darling Lana,' said Briar Rose. 'I knew I could depend on you.' She nodded at Harrison. 'Both of you. Now climb on my back, quick sticks. There's no time to lose.'

Chapter Eighteen

As wide and wild as it looked from the bank, the river was unimaginably broad and treacherous close up. But Briar Rose was more than equal to the task, powering through the rushing water like a steamboat, her giant wings and elegant neck sheltering the two children from the spray, while her enormous webbed feet pounded the fast-moving currents beneath.

As they neared the opposite bank, a crooked wooden jetty sprang into view. Bobbing alongside it was the witch's boat.

Before they knew it, the swan was in the shallows, and nudging them off her back with her beak.

'We're here,' urged Briar Rose. 'Behind the jetty is a stream. Follow the stream, and you'll get to the witch's cottage.'

'Aren't you coming with us?' asked Lana.

Briar Rose shook her head. 'I can't leave the water.'

'Why not?' asked Harrison.

'The witch's magic won't let me. I've tried so many times, but the second I step on dry land, I find myself back at the bottom of the river, drowning. Then I swim to the surface, and the whole thing starts all over again. I'm trapped.'

'But why would the witch cast such a horrible spell?' asked Lana.

Briar Rose shrugged. 'I have no idea. To punish me, I suppose. Now hurry. All that matters is you get to Hansel and Gretel before it's too late.'

'We'll find them,' said Lana, hugging the swan one last time. 'As soon as this horn dries out, we'll blow on it, the prince will come, and you'll all be together again.'

'Promise?' asked Briar Rose.

'Promise,' added Harrison, joining the hug.

Then he and Lana splashed out of the shallows and up the bank, pulling on handfuls of wild grass to help them reach the top. Then they scurried alongside the stream, Lana in front, Harrison behind, as it carved across a stone-strewn meadow, before plunging into the dappled shade of the silver birch forest.

They ran in silence as the grass at the water's edge gave way to fern, which then gave way to bare earth.

'Sorry,' said Lana, over her shoulder. 'For saying you were boring for working so hard.'

'That's okay.'

'It's good you know about levers and stuff.'

'Thanks,' panted Harrison. The forest floor was steepening, as the little stream weaved its way ahead of them. 'And I'm sorry that I stopped playing with you, and for saying that you were making things up. When we get home, things will be different, I promise.'

He expected Lana to turn and flash a smile. But instead, she stopped running.

'What?' asked Harrison.

'The stream. It's gone.'

A few metres ahead of them, the babbling water sunk between two large grey lichen-covered boulders, then was no more. Which way should they go?

'Maybe we should climb a tree, see if we can see the cottage?' asked Harrison.

'How? There are no low branches.'

It was true. Everywhere they looked, slender white tree trunks towered above them, propping up a shimmering canopy of green leaves. Even if they stood on one another's shoulders, they'd never be able to reach.

'That's weird,' said Harrison.

'What is?'

'Listen. No birds.'

'Wait.' Lana put her finger to her lips. 'I

can hear water!' Then suddenly she was off, bounding up the hillside, giving Harrison no choice but to follow. As he hauled himself up over an outcrop of rock, he was greeted by the sight of Lana standing proudly at the head of a miniature waterfall.

'This way!' she called, and disappeared from view.

Harrison took a deep breath and scrambled up past the waterfall, onto a plateau. Lana was standing at its furthermost edge with her back to him, looking out. She gestured for him to be quiet, and he crept up beside her.

Below them was an enormous wooden watermill, its giant wheel turning slowly in the stream. A rickety house next to it was surrounded by playground rides of all shapes and sizes: a carousel of brightly coloured horses; a swingboat, rocking back and forth, and a steam-train, circling in a figure of eight, each powered by an eccentric system of pistons, bands and pulleys.

Even stranger, Lana and Harrison could hear voices. Children's voices. And they were laughing.

Chapter Nineteen

'Gretel, stop! STOP!'

'Don't be such a baby, Hansel!'

Hansel and Gretel's voices rang out across the dell, then collapsed in a fit of giggles. They seemed to be coming from high up, behind the house.

Lana and Harrison looked at one another Was this some sort of trick? Where was the witch?

'Look!' whispered Lana. A narrow gangway led from beside the stream all the way up to the front of the house.

Harrison gave her hand a comforting squeeze and together they made their way through the ferns, towards it.

'Faster, Hansel! FASTER!'

'I can't! My legs are hurting!'

Softly and silently, Lana climbed, with Harrison close behind her, pausing every few seconds, looking for any sign of the witch. But the house appeared to be empty. They could see now that the decking around the house was crowded with plant pots. Lana turned and nodded at Harrison, and the two of them noiselessly mounted the last few steps. No sooner had they done so than they heard more laughter, coming from somewhere behind the house.

'Gretel, watch!'

'I can't, I've got my eyes closed!'

As fast as they could, Lana and Harrison made a crouched run to the porch of the cabin, then ran along its front wall, ducking beneath an open window, in case the witch was inside. Then they raced along the side wall to the back of the house and peered into the garden.

It was magical. There were planters overflowing with sweet-smelling rosemary and lavender, neat rows of mouth-watering lettuce, and bright-green vines dripping with cherry tomatoes and broad beans. And in the centre of a small circle of green lawn, surrounded by apple trees, two children were playing on a see-saw.

'Higher! Higher!' shouted Gretel.

'I'm trying!' bellowed Hansel.

Lana couldn't help grinning. Briar Rose's children were safe! She glanced up at the house. The windows showed no signs of life, and the side door was closed. She nudged Harrison, and the two of them wove their way across the deck towards the apple trees, then ducked down behind a barrel.

'Hansel! Gretel!' called Lana, in as loud a voice as she dared.

But Hansel and Gretel were far too busy with their game to take any notice.

'Come on, you weakling!' hooted Gretel.

'I'm not a weakling!' barked Hansel.

'*PSSST!*' hissed Lana. But on the other side of the apple trees, the see-saw kept swinging.

'Are so!' taunted Gretel.

'Am not!'

After one last wary glance back at the house, Lana led Harrison under the bows of the nearest apple tree, and onto the lawn.

As soon as they were out in the open, it was clear that something wasn't right. Now that Hansel and Gretel were not half hidden by leaves, Lana could see that they weren't Briar Rose's children at all . . . They were painted wooden statues!

Lana felt a stabbing pain as sharp fingers gripped her left earlobe!

'Got you!' sneered a familiar voice, and as she twisted and turned to free herself, Lana realised her captor was the little old man! He was back in his maroon supermarket boiler suit, and with his other hand he had hold of

Harrison's earlobe too!

'*Ow!*' winced Lana. 'Let me go! You're hurting me!'

'*You're hurting me!*' mimicked the little old man, copying Hansel's voice exactly. 'Don't be such a baby!' he said, in a perfect imitation of Gretel. Then he burst into gales of laughter, somehow managing to sound like both children at the same time.

'Let go!' growled Harrison, trying to twist out of his grip, but the little old man's strength was far greater than his small frame suggested.

'Trust me,' he leered, 'this is nothing compared to what my mistress has planned. You wait till she gets home.' Then he marched them across the deck, kicked open the back door and dragged them into the darkness of the cabin!

A domed cage made of birch twigs was just visible by the light of the fire. Its door was open and the little old man threw Harrison inside. Then he took the hunting horn from Lana's neck.

'I'll take this,' he grinned. Then he flung Lana in too, slammed the door and bolted it shut.

'That's mine!' demanded Lana. 'Give it back!'

'Pretty little thing, isn't it?' said the little old man, as he examined the hunting horn. 'Where did you get it, I wonder?'

'Where are Hansel and Gretel?' asked Harrison.

The little old man smiled a sickly smile. 'You just saw them.'

'Those were statues,' said Lana. 'The witch has taken them prisoner, hasn't she?'

'Taken them?' echoed the little old man. 'Not yet. But I'm sure she will soon. With parsley sauce, I expect.'

As he spoke, there was a rattling sound, and a cloud of steam belched out of the lid of a large cauldron that was heating over the fire.

'My mistress loves children, you see. And thanks to me, she now has a constant supply.'

He put some more wood on the fire, then picked up the empty log basket and headed for the door.

'What do you mean?' asked Lana.

The little old man paused. 'Seriously? Surely you've worked it out by now?'

Lana shook her head.

'You see, here in the world of fairytales we

are running out of children. Too many hungry witches, and too few of the little snitches to go around. But in your world there's children galore! So I – if I say so myself – had a rather ingenious idea—'

'The supermarket,' said Harrison.

'Don't interrupt.' The little old man shot Harrison a withering look. 'As I was saying, I had a rather ingenious idea. Bring children from your world into ours. Once you were here you'd be powerless against my mistress's magic. So, I persuaded my mistress to build a portal. And this is the really clever bit . . .' He started to snigger. 'I decided to hide it in a—'

'Supermarket,' said Lana.

'WOULD YOU PLEASE STOP DOING THAT!' shouted the little old man. 'But yes, in a supermarket. Low prices to reel in the parents, and stories to hook the children.'

'But . . .' protested Lana, trying to make sense of this. 'You kept telling me *not* to read the story because it was too scary.'

'Exactly,' countered the little old man, fixing her with his beady brown eyes. 'How else do you get silly children to do what you want?'

'But wait,' interrupted Harrison. 'Why take us to all those other bits of the story? Why not bring us straight here?'

The little old man grinned. 'Why do you think?'

Harrison shrugged.

'To make you brave. If you'd come straight here, you'd have been terrified. And my mistress would hate that. She says it affects the taste.'

'You're lying!' said Lana.

'And you're supper!' gloated the little old man. 'First, she'll turn you both into wood, like she did Hansel and Gretel. Best way to keep you fresh, she says. Then when she's good and ready, she'll boil you in that pot and eat you.'

Then he left, closing the door behind him.

'Quick!' hissed Lana, rattling the door of the cage. 'We've got to get out of here!'

But the door wouldn't budge.

'See if you can reach the bolt!' urged Harrison. But Lana could only get the tips of her fingers through the gaps between the bars of the cage.

'It's too narrow!'

'What are we going to do?' he gulped.

'We have to stay calm.'

'She's going to eat us! The witch is going to come back, and then she's going to eat us!'

'HARRISON!' Lana gripped her brother by the shoulders. He stared at her with eyes like saucers. 'Remember our mission. We're here to save Hansel and Gretel. Somehow, we have to get out of this cage!'

'How are we going to do that?' asked Harrison, a note of despair in his voice. Everything he'd studied hadn't prepared him for this particular problem.

Lana's mind was blank. She had no idea how they would escape. But then a thought struck her. It was risky, but it just might work.

'When he comes back, ask me to tell you a story,' said Lana.

But that was all she had time to say, because

at that moment the door flew open, and in came the little old man, struggling with a heavy basket of logs.

Lana watched him work in silence, choosing her moment. Her heart was racing, but she was determined not to show it.

'I have to admit,' said Lana, doing her best to sound as casual as possible. 'The supermarket, the pick 'n' mix, hooking us in with fairytales . . . it really was very clever.'

The little old man gave her a suspicious glance, then threw a couple more logs on the fire.

'The witch is going to be so pleased with you.'

There was a pause, while the little old man prodded the flames with a poker.

'When is she coming back?'

'Never you mind.'

'Lana?' Harrison pleaded. 'Please will you tell me a story, to take my mind off the witch?'

'Oh, very well,' said Lana, pretending to be cross. 'Just a quick one.'

'Can it be a fairytale?'

The little old man pricked up his ears.

'Of course,' replied Lana. 'Now, let me think . . .'

Lana pretended to think, but all the time she was watching the little old man closely. He was stirring the cauldron, but Lana could tell that he was listening.

'I know,' she said, in a confident voice, 'what about *The Little Boy, the Little Girl, and the Little Old Man*?'

'Oh, yes please,' said Harrison. 'I love that one.'

Of course, Harrison had no idea what Lana

was talking about.

'Now, how does it start?' mused Lana. 'Ah, yes . . .'

And this . . . well, this is pretty much what she told him . . .

Chapter Twenty

Once there was a little boy and a little girl whose father died suddenly, leaving them and their mother all alone in the world.

To begin with, their mother was very upset and cried day and night but, as time went by, eventually she was able to smile when she thought about the wonderful times they had shared as a family.

More time passed, and their mother decided it was time to get married again. One day, while she was gathering firewood in the forest, she met a little old man wearing extremely fashionable purple clothes, and shortly after she decided to marry him.

Lana saw the little old man pause as he put another log on the fire. She smiled to herself, knowing that everyone loves a story where they can see themselves as one of the characters.

A year after they were married, the couple had a baby daughter.

'Don't worry,' the little old man reassured his wife. 'Just because we have our own child, I won't forget about my stepchildren. I'll treat all our children just the same.'

But he didn't. Instead, he spoiled his own daughter and was often mean to the little boy and girl. Whenever something broke, he made sure they got the blame, getting them into so much trouble that even their mother started to believe his lies.

While his daughter had a feather bed in her very own room, the little boy and girl were forced to live in a cage in the kitchen and given hardly anything to eat. Soon they were so miserable that they decided to run away.

'But where will we go?' the little girl asked her brother.

'The forest,' he answered. 'It's dark and full of dangerous creatures, but even so it has to be better than here.'

That night, they waited until the rest of

the house were asleep and then the little girl slipped her hand through the bars of the cage, undid the bolt and together they crept out of their house and into the forest.

Now, what the two children didn't know was that the little old man had magical powers. And when their mother had met him in the forest, he had cast a spell to make her fall in love with him. The little old man was as ugly on the outside as he was inside, but his spell had made their mother believe him to be kindhearted and handsome.

Lana had to stop herself from grinning as she saw the little old man frown. He had forgotten all about the fire, and was now leaning forward on his stool, listening carefully to her story.

Like many people who understand magic, the little old man could see with his eyes closed, so even though he was asleep he could see the children creeping out of the house.

'Ha!' He thought, '*Now I can be rid of my horrible stepchildren once and for all!*' And he cast a spell on all the streams of the forest, so that anyone who drank from them would be turned into a deer. And, with the forest full of hunters, the children would never be safe.

Meanwhile, in the depths of the forest, the little boy and girl came across a babbling brook.

'Look!' exclaimed the boy. 'Let's drink! We've been walking for hours and I'm so thirsty!'

But as they both leant down to the river, the little girl heard the water whispering.

'*Don't drink me!*' it said. '*I am enchanted*

so that anyone who sips from me will turn into a deer!'

The little girl turned quickly to her brother. 'No! Don't drink the water!'

But it was too late. The little boy was gone, and in his place was a startled white fawn!

'Sister, sister, what's happening to me?' he cried.

'Hush, little fawn,' said the girl, taking care not to make any sudden moves that might scare the animal away. 'I'll look after you.'

Lana paused. Much to her delight, the little old man was hanging on her every word.

The girl led the fawn through the forest and soon she began to tire. But she couldn't find anywhere for her and the fawn to safely rest.

233

Soon her legs were aching so badly she felt as if she couldn't take another step. She was just about to bed down on the forest floor, when the little white fawn gently nudged her arm and led her through the trees towards a clearing, in the middle of which was a house!

It was beautiful! It had a pretty thatched roof and honey-coloured stone walls and a garden full of brightly coloured flowers and neat rows of delicious-looking vegetables.

When the little girl tried the front door, she found it unlocked, and so she led the fawn inside.

'Hello!' she called. 'Is anyone home?' But no one answered. 'Come, dear brother,' she said to the fawn. 'Let's look after this house until the owner returns, and hopefully they will be kind enough to let us stay.'

She gathered some tasty treats from the garden, cooked a midnight feast and then, both exhausted, they fell into a blissful sleep.

And they might have lived there happily ever after, if the next morning they hadn't been rudely awoken by a loud hunting horn!

'Harrison, do you know what a hunting horn is?' asked Lana. She gave Harrison a meaningful stare.

'No. What's a hunting horn?' asked Harrison, playing along.

'One of these,' barked the little old man impatiently, holding up the horn he had taken from Lana. 'Now, come on, what happened next?'

'Show him properly,' demanded Lana. 'This may be the last story he ever hears.

Maybe stand it on the stove, so it's much closer?'

The little old man sighed and set the horn down on the cast-iron stove above the fire.

Her plan was working! *The stove will dry the horn*, thought Lana. And so she carried on . . .

On hearing the hunting horn, the fawn sprang up from his sleep.

'Listen, sister!' cried the fawn. 'Can you hear that sound? It's the hunters! Let them chase me, please!'

'What?' asked the girl. 'Why would you want them to hunt you?'

'Please! I need to run!'

'Very well,' said the little girl. 'But when you come back, you must knock three times and say: "Open the door, sister dear, for your brother fawn is here!" Then I will know it is you.'

The little girl opened the window, and the white fawn sprang out, over the garden fence, and after the huntsmen. All day long he taunted them, staying just out of range of their arrows. Then, as night fell, he trotted back to the cottage.

Just as the girl had told him, he knocked three times with his hoof and called out: 'Open the door, sister dear, for your brother fawn is here!'

The little girl flung open the door and threw her arms round his neck.

'Thank goodness you're safe!' she cried. Then she led him inside, gave him his supper and they curled up to sleep, she in her feather bed, and he on his pile of hay beside her.

But the next morning, they were once again woken by the sound of a hunting horn.

'A what?' asked Harrison. Even in the darkness of the cage, Lana could see a twinkle in his eye.

'I already told you,' said Lana, pretending to be annoyed. '*A hunting horn.*'

'Of course,' said Harrison, 'Like the one on the stove.'

'*Sssh!*' said the little old man. 'Stop interrupting.'

'Please let me go with the hunters again!' exclaimed the fawn.

'Absolutely not!' said his sister. 'You were lucky last time. But it's too dangerous.'

'Please!' begged the fawn.

The girl felt she had no choice but to let him go, and once again he went bounding off through the forest to join the hunt.

But this time he *wasn't* so lucky. The head huntsman shot an arrow in his leg, and though the fawn still managed to limp back to the house, the huntsman tracked him and then watched from the bushes as the little fawn knocked three times and called out, 'Open the door, sister dear, for your your brother fawn is here!'

The girl opened the door and ushered the fawn inside.

Hmm . . . thought the huntsman. *So that's where he lives! A snow-white fawn! Very unusual. What a prize his head would make, stuffed and mounted on the palace wall! I'm going to tell the king about this.*

And he snuck away without being seen.

When the girl saw that her brother was wounded, she was overcome with worry. 'That's your last hunt,' she said as she bandaged his leg, wrapping it with herbs from the garden. 'It is too dangerous.'

'But you don't understand!' pleaded her brother. 'Every drop of my blood yearns to run!'

That night the little girl was so worried she hardly slept.

Sure enough, as dawn broke, they heard the horn again.

'Have you ever heard a hunting horn?' Lana asked Harrison, giving him another pointed look.

'Oh, will you both stop interrupting!' said

the little old man crossly.

'Well, I'm sorry, but we're just trying to get into the story,' said Harrison. 'I've never heard a hunting horn before.'

Unable to contain his annoyance, the little old man snatched the prince's horn from the stove and blew. Much to the children's delight, a rich and deep tone echoed out of the cottage and across the forest. 'It sounds like that! All right? Satisfied? Now, Lana, tell us what happened to the fawn?'

Harrison and Lana looked at one another. Lana's plan had worked, the little old man had blown the horn! Now they just had to hope the prince had heard it and came in time . . .

'Well?' demanded the little old man.

'Sorry,' said Lana, expecting the prince to

arrive at any minute. 'Where was I?'

'The huntsman has discovered where the fawn lives.'

'Ah, yes,' said Lana. She glanced towards the door.

'Then get on with it,' snarled the little old man.

Lana cleared her throat and continued with the story.

Sure enough, as dawn broke, the horn sounded again. The fawn's wound had miraculously healed, and once more he bounded off through the forest, eager to join the hunt.

But the king had now been told of the fawn and had other plans. He had ordered the hunters to chase, but not fire. And while the fawn was running through the forest, the king paid a visit to the cottage.

He knocked three times on the door as he had been instructed by the head huntsman, and then called out: 'Open the door, sister dear, for your brother fawn is here!'

The door opened, and—

Suddenly, the latch of the cottage clicked, and the back door swung open.

Lana and Harrison sat up, beaming, ready to greet the prince!

Then their faces fell.

Because towering in the doorway, wrapped in a purple-and-gold silk cloak, was the witch.

Chapter Twenty-One

The witch pulled back the hood of her cloak. Her skin was as smooth as china, her hair like flax, and her eyes sparkled like rubies.

She sniffed the air. 'Rumpolt, has it ever occurred to you why I live in a remote forest?'

The little old man gulped in fear and shook his head. 'House prices?'

'It's because I value my privacy.' She closed the door, as if to emphasise her point. 'You understand what privacy is, don't you?'

The little old man nodded, too scared to speak.

'Then what, may I ask, was that dreadful noise?'

The little old man looked down at the horn round his neck. His lower lip trembled, as if he was about to cry. Then he thrust out an accusing finger. 'It's their fault.'

Ever so slowly, the witch turned and peered at Harrison and Lana, seeing them for the first time. She smiled, closed her eyes and breathed deeply, as if the air was full of delicious scent.

'Goodness me!' she cooed. 'Children!'

'From the supermarket,' simpered the

little old man, wringing his hands, his eyes begging for forgiveness. 'I told you that my plan would work. These two are the first of many, mistress, I promise.'

'But what are they doing in there? That's no way to treat guests.'

'I . . . I . . .' stammered the little old man.

'I do apologise,' soothed the witch, unbolting the cage. 'Honestly, Rumpolt, what were you thinking?'

She offered her hand to Lana, who hesitated.

'Come, child. I won't bite, I promise.'

Warily, Lana took the witch's hand, and let herself be led out into the room. But instead of letting her go, the witch pulled her closer.

'And what might your name be?'

'Lana.'

The witch's fingers brushed Lana's cheek. They were ice cold, and Lana felt herself shudder.

'And who's this?' she peered into the cage.

'My brother. Harrison.'

'A boy!' beamed the witch. 'Come, let's take a look at you.' Hesitantly, Harrison climbed out of the cage and stood beside his sister.

'Now, were you offered a drink? Or anything to eat?'

Lana and Harrison shook their heads.

'Rumpolt, some food for our guests!' She threw a meaningful look at the little old man, who nodded and set to work at the stove.

'Here, have a drink,' the witch smiled at the children as she picked up a pewter jug and filled two tin cups with steaming, thick hot chocolate.

As delicious as the chocolate smelled, they knew better than to take a drink offered by a witch. They each took a cup and lifted it to their lips, pretending to sip.

'Now, Rumpolt, where are those pancakes? It never does for children to be too thin, I always think. Every child ta—' The witch cut herself off, mid-sentence. 'I'm sorry, *looks* better, with a little fat on them.'

'At your service, mistress,' said the little old man breathlessly, offering up two delicious-looking pancakes drenched in syrup.

'Yum!' exclaimed the witch, rubbing her hands with glee. 'Harrison, why don't you take one?'

Harrison looked at Lana and gave her

the tiniest of nods that only a sister could understand.

Harrison gingerly reached out his hand, hovering over the pancakes, as if he was trying to choose one. But, quick as a flash, he turned and threw his drink into the little old man's face, who shrieked in surprise.

A second later, Lana threw her drink at the witch!

'Eurgghh!' spluttered the witch, stumbling backwards as the thick liquid dripped down her face.

Lana leapt around and pushed the witch into the open cage. Before the little old man had composed himself, Harrison grabbed him tightly by the ear and threw him in the cage, too!

Lana hurriedly bolted the cage, then the

two children raced for the door . . .

They froze.

Standing right in front of them was the witch. How had she gotten out so quickly?

'Impressive,' she simpered. 'Most children are too terrified to try to escape. But you two . . .' She licked her thin lips. 'You two are different. Well done. Rumpolt, fetch their reward, please.'

Lana and Harrison turned round to see the little old man standing next to the now-empty cage. Their hearts sank: the witch's magic was too powerful for them to overcome. All they could do was watch helplessly, as the little old man sauntered over to a large glass-fronted cabinet. In it were row after row of tiny glass phials, each one full of coloured powder, and decorated with strange symbols.

'I think the green, don't you?' asked the witch, and the little old man dutifully handed her a little glass phial of powder. Smiling, the witch pulled out the cork stopper, tipped a few grains into the palm of her hand, then sprinkled them over Harrison's and Lana's heads.

Lana glanced across at Harrison and saw to her horror that he had been turned into a wooden statue! She tried to speak, but couldn't move her lips. She couldn't move her head either, or her eyes, or any other part of her body. Suddenly it dawned on her. She was a statue too!

'You're probably wondering why you can't move. You've been turned into wood, to keep you fresh. Rumpolt?'

The little old man edged into view.

'The girl can go outside with the others. The boy . . .' The witch brushed Harrison's painted wooden cheek with yellow fingers. 'The boy can go in the pot.'

'Yes, mistress.'

'*No!*' Lana yelled in her mind. '*Let him go!*' But again no words came out. All she could do was watch in horror as the little old man dragged Harrison out of her eyeline.

Lana heard the lid of the cauldron being lifted, and the hiss and spit of the boiling water. Every part of her wanted to kick and punch and fight, to do anything she could to help her brother, but she couldn't move a muscle.

The witch walked towards the cauldron and out of Lana's line of sight. Now all Lana could see was an empty corner of the room!

'In he goes!' shouted the little old man. And then Lana heard huffing and puffing, as if someone was struggling with a heavy weight . . .

Then . . . *Zswing!*

The sound of an arrow!

Immediately followed by a blood-curdling scream!

Chapter Twenty-Two

The very next moment, Lana found she could move. She spun to face the cauldron, but instead of seeing Harrison in the pot, much to her relief her brother had also transformed back to his usual self. And next to him, the little old man was staring in shock.

Looking down, Lana saw the outline of

the witch, face down on the floor, covered by her silk cloak. Sticking up out of the cloak was a single golden arrow.

The little old man raised both hands in surrender. Lana followed his gaze to the open door. Standing beyond it was the prince, holding his longbow.

Prince Otto *had* heard the horn and come to the rescue, just in the nick of time!

'Lana? Are you all right?' he asked, rushing to her side. 'I came as soon as I could.'

Suddenly there was the sound of beating wings, and a giant swan landed in the doorway.

'Briar Rose!' exclaimed Lana.

But instead of greeting them, the swan thumped across the wooden floor, snatching up the witch's silk cloak to reveal that her body had disappeared! Instead, right where

the witch had been lying, there was a large frog with ruby-red eyes.

'It's the witch!' called Harrison. 'She's still alive!'

No sooner had he spoken, when the frog made a leap for the open window.

But the swan was too quick for it. With a single beat of its wings, it launched itself into the air, knocking the frog upwards with a strike of its beak, then opening its mouth wide, so that the helpless amphibian plunged straight down its gullet.

Then the swan swallowed, shook its head, and everyone watched as a frog-shaped lump travelled all the way down its neck and disappeared into its stomach.

'Eww,' said Lana, both delighted and really grossed out.

No sooner had it regained its composure, than the swan began to change shape. Its legs grew longer, its body thinner, and its neck shorter. Its wings became a white cloak, and Briar Rose emerged in human form.

'The witch is gone,' smiled Briar Rose, and Lana saw that her eyes were flecked with red. 'And she can never hurt us again.'

'Mama!' called two familiar voices.

'Children!' cried Briar Rose, kneeling and throwing her arms wide.

Hansel and Gretel sprinted towards their mother and Briar Rose hugged them tight.

'I . . . I . . . don't understand . . .?' stammered the prince, astonished. 'What are you two doing here?'

'The witch kidnapped us,' said Gretel.

'What?!'

'She turned us into statues,' explained Hansel. 'She was going to eat us. These children tried to save us, but she turned them into statues too.'

Briar Rose looked up at the prince. 'That witch you just killed was the thirteenth fairy.'

'*The* thirteenth fairy?'

'Exactly. She tricked us. She sent me a letter, pretending to be your father. But now she's dead, her magic is transferring to me.'

But Harrison wasn't smiling. 'Lana . . .' His voice trailed away.

'What?'

'Where's Rumpolt?'

He was right. The little old man, who

had been standing beside the cauldron, had completely vanished.

Frowning, Lana rushed over. But all that was left was his discarded maroon boiler suit.

Then something caught Lana's eye. The witch's cabinet was open, and a little brown bird was sitting on top of it. In its beak was a small glass phial, dangling from a ribbon. The powder inside was gold, and the ribbon was purple.

Lana gasped. Suddenly it all fell into place: the little brown bird and the little old man were one and the same!

The bird turned its head sideways, looking directly at Lana. It chirruped, then took off, swooping over everyone's heads, and out of the door.

'He's getting away!' Lana exclaimed. 'That

little bird who just flew off, that's him!' A dreadful thought dawned on her. 'I think he's going to shut the portal!'

'Quick!' said Briar Rose, as she began to change back into a swan. 'Climb aboard!' Soon her transformation was complete, and Harrison and Lana clambered onto her back.

'Children,' announced Briar Rose to Hansel and Gretel. 'A fond farewell to our good friends Lana and Harrison. We owe them our lives!' And with that, she flapped her giant wings and took off, soaring up over the lip of the dell, then plunging down into the valley.

'Bye, Lana! Bye, Harrison!' The children's voices rang out among the trees. 'Good luck!'

But Harrison and Lana were far too focused on clinging on to call back. Tree trunks flashed silver on either side of them, missing them by inches, as Briar Rose glided onward and downward, skirting the maze of rocks at the foot of the waterfall, and on into the forest.

Within minutes they were flying above the stream, heading for the river. Looking up, Lana saw the little brown bird just ahead of them, still carrying the phial, flying for all it was worth. But Briar Rose's strength was mighty and they were gaining on it!

'*Kraaak!*' called Briar Rose.

The little brown bird, sensing that it was losing the race, veered left into the trees.

'That way!' called Lana, pointing after it.

'No,' replied Briar Rose. 'We'll follow the stream; it's quicker!'

Sure enough, a few seconds later they broke out of the forest, and Lana glimpsed the little

'Briar Rose glided onward and downward.'

brown bird some two hundred metres ahead of them.

'Quick!' Lana called. 'He's heading for the portal!'

Briar Rose steered left, leaving the stream behind them, and began to race across marshland, gaining on the little bird with every beat of her wings. But then, disaster! A rogue gust of wind caught them, blowing them way off course.

'There!' called Lana, pointing to the river. The little brown bird was circling above the water, as if it was searching for something. Then it dived beneath the surface and disappeared.

Briar Rose battled the wind, but there was nothing she could do but climb up out of the path of the gust, into the stiller air above.

'That must be where the portal is!' said Lana, pointing to the spot where the bird had dived.

'Hold on!' ordered Briar Rose. She launched herself forwards and began to glide down towards the river.

Lana and Harrison gripped onto Briar Rose's feathers, desperately trying to hang on. Soon the water was rushing up to meet them, as Briar Rose's legs skated through the fast-moving currents at the centre of the river. Then, once she was sure they were safe, Briar Rose slowed to a stop and settled on the surface.

'Here!' she called out, stretching her wings. Lana clung to one, and Harrison to the other. 'Deep breath!'

Lana filled her lungs with air, just as Briar Rose turned back into human form and dived!

Everything went silent as they sank, deeper and deeper. Lana opened her eyes and saw the surface of the water way above her, glimmering in the sunlight. She felt the blood rush to her face, as she longed to breathe out. Then, just when she couldn't hold on a second longer, the water fell away, her breath exploded outwards, and she took in a huge lungful of air.

It took a few moments for her to realise that she, Briar Rose, and Harrison were bobbing like corks inside the clear plastic chute.

'Found it!' exclaimed Briar Rose. 'I was about to give up.'

Lana tried to speak but couldn't catch her breath.

'You need to climb,' urged Briar Rose.

The water was rising fast and it wouldn't

be long until the tunnel was flooded.

'Lana, you first,' instructed Briar Rose. 'Climb on my shoulders and I'll give you a push.'

Still struggling for breath, her wet arms and legs slipping and sliding on the smooth plastic, Lana did as she was told.

'Now stand up!' called Briar Rose.

Using her arms as a brace, Lana wobbled up into a standing position.

'Go on! Climb!'

'I can't!' called Lana. 'It's too slippy!'

'Okay,' said Briar Rose. 'You're going to have to jump. Crouch down, then throw yourself up!'

Lana put her hands on the top of Briar Rose's head and crouched as low as she could. Then, summoning all her strength, she leapt up into the chute!

For an awful moment she hovered in mid-air . . .

Then, ever-so-slowly, she began to rise . . .

She glanced down at Briar Rose and Harrison, who was already climbing up after her.

'Goodbye!' she called to Briar Rose.

'Goodbye, Lana!' Briar Rose beamed a smile as bright as the sun. 'And thank you!'

Lana looked up – or was it down? – as the walls of the chute began to slide past her, faster and faster, until she wasn't sure if she was rising or falling. She could hear the thundering rush of water, gushing up the chute behind her, almost upon her. Then she was most definitely falling: down, down, down, faster and faster, backwards, forwards, and sideways, as the tunnel began to twist and turn! Just when she felt she couldn't go any faster, it corkscrewed round and round, slowing her almost to a halt. Her head hit a trapdoor, which instantly gave way, and she opened her eyes to find herself poking out of the mint imperials tub.

Lana gasped at the destruction around her – a huge crack had opened up, running the entire length of the supermarket, and it was growing in size by the second, swallowing whatever it came into contact with.

She'd barely taken in the chaos surrounding her when she was propelled out of the tub and landed with a hard thump on the floor. Harrison's head appeared above her, but before he could say anything a jet of water thrust him out of the tub and he landed next to Lana with another hard thump.

They'd made it to the supermarket, but they were far from safe.

They leapt to their feet as the crevasse grew even longer, swallowing the entire toy aisle to their right. The ground was shaking and rumbling and there was a terrifying crunch as the steel girder holding up the roof began to buckle.

The whole place was about to collapse.

'That way!' yelled Lana, pointing towards the front of the store. She held out her hand, Harrison took it, and they ran for their lives.

Lana glanced back to see pick 'n' mix tubs teetering on the edge of the chasm, showering sweets into the depths, before the whole rack plunged downwards. The portals were closing forever.

Lana and Harrison ran for all they were worth, heading for the double entrance doors on the other side of the tills.

But Lana halted in her tracks, Harrison slamming into her. A red light was flashing and the electronic doors were opening and shutting rhythmically, directly over the crevasse, which now stretched out into the car park. Lana spun round, hoping there was another way out, but the whole building was folding in on itself. This was their only hope.

'We have to jump!' yelled Harrison.

We'll never make it! Lana thought.

But Harrison was right, it was their only choice. So, Lana let all the fear drain from her body, filling it with still and calm. Time slowed to a trickle. She took a deep breath, focusing on the rhythm of the doors: open, close, open, close. She took a few measured steps backward, then sprinted forward . . . The doors closed just as she planted her left foot on the lip of the crevasse and jumped! She sailed through the air as the doors began to open, reaching the middle once they were as wide as they could go. Then, as they started to close, she began to descend, landing firmly on her right foot on the other side.

She glanced back and saw Harrison mid-leap in the doorway, but he had mis-timed his jump and Lana watched helplessly as the double doors closed on her brother's trailing foot, and he began to fall. Straining every muscle, Harrison twisted his upper body and threw out his arms, reaching for the edge.

'Help!' screamed Harrison, clinging on with his fingertips.

Lana threw herself down to the ground and grabbed hold of his wrists.

A mushroom cloud of dust billowed up into the night air as the building collapsed in a heap.

'I'm going to fall!' bellowed Harrison. 'Lana, I'm going to fall!'

Epilogue

'D on't worry!' shouted Lana. 'I've got you!'

She leaned back and pulled, feeling every muscle in her body strain and burn. Slowly but surely, she lifted him higher and higher, until he was sitting beside her in the treehouse.

'Sorry!' exclaimed Harrison. 'I nearly lost it there.'

'Don't worry,' said Lana, reassuringly. 'It's okay to be scared in a game. That way if you're ever in real danger, you know what to do.'

'Thanks, Lana,' he said, gratefully. 'Now. Where were we?'

'I'm me,' Lana reminded him. 'And you're you. The supermarket is collapsing, and we're trying to escape."

'Harrison! Lana!'

Their father was calling them.

'Lunchtime!'

'Five more minutes!' shouted Harrison. 'We're in the middle of a game.'

'Now, please,' called their father. 'The food's on the table.'

'At least they're playing together again,' said their mother, joining him. The sun was still shining, despite the threatening clouds, and they had decided to eat outside.

'True,' said their father, filling four glasses from the water jug. 'Although I think I preferred it when Harrison spent all day in his room. Less noisy.' Then he grinned, to show he didn't really mean it.

'You know what I think it is?'

'What?'

'That book of fairytales. The one we got from Grimm's. It's fired their imaginations.'

Their father set the jug down and shrugged. 'At least something good came out of that place, before the council demolished it.'

'Do you really think that's what happened?'

'No planning permission is my guess,' he said. 'Why else would it disappear overnight?'

But that was as far as their conversation

got, because at that moment, it began to rain. Lana and Harrison came running over, laughing and giggling, and their mother began shouting orders about which things to bring in, while their father tried to shield the table with an umbrella.

Which meant none of them saw the little brown bird perched in the juniper tree, watching them with its beady brown eyes.

Deciding it had seen enough, the little brown bird chirruped a farewell, and took off across the garden. Up over the roof it flew, and down the hill towards the village: soaring high over the shop and the red post box; swooping down over the hollyhock gardens beside the row of crooked houses; then skimming the high yew hedge of Hilcot House.

Then, as the rain came tipping down, it made the turn out onto the empty common. Where there had once been an enormous supermarket, there was now just churned-up earth that was rapidly turning to mud.

The little brown bird circled the common, as if it was searching for something. And then it saw it: a sign, half buried in the ground. It was purple, with gold letters which read 'GRI' and then stopped, because the rest of the word was underground.

As the bird hovered, watching with beady eyes, the sign began to sink into the mud. Soon there was just one gold-and-purple corner left: then there was nothing.

The mud belched, as if was digesting a tasty morsel of food.

Satisfied, the little brown bird chirruped

once more, beat its wings and began to head up, up, up through the driving rain, to where the sun was breaking beyond the clouds.

Acknowledgements

Once upon a time, in a land far away, I set out to write a story for each of my three children, where they are the main character. *The Night I Met Father Christmas* features my oldest son, Jackson, and *The Boy Who Made the World Disappear* has a leading role for my middle child, Harrison. This third book is for Lana, my daughter. Like her brothers before her, she has patiently listened to early versions and suggested many helpful changes. Also, like them, I hope she doesn't change her mind and sue me when she's older ...

I fell into a fairytale of my own when I met my wife, Jessica Parker. Jess, thank you for bringing Lana and Harrison into the world and for being the most brilliant mother and homemaker, as well as a full-time creative badass in film and fashion. Also for getting us great tables in restaurants when they confuse you with Sarah Jessica Parker.

A big part of the thrill of writing these stories is working with Daniela Terrazzini. As ever, she has surpassed herself to create illustrations that are timeless, magical, and ever-so-slightly creepy. I am convinced Daniela has a portal of her own where she goes to get them drawn. A bit like one of Damien Hirst's factories but in fairyland rather than Stroud. But I digress ...

I have really fallen on my feet with Rachel Denwood's crack Children's team at Simon and Schuster, led from the front by Ali Dougal. My editor Jane Griffiths helped breathe life into the story, not least by coming up with a much better title (I went for *The Enchanted Supermarket*, which on reflection sounds weird, and not in a good way). Sam Swinnerton drew all of the story threads together when it counted most, and produced a crystal-clear copy-edit and elegant layout, and Lowri Ribbons and Anna Bowles provided elevating proofreads. David McDougall is responsible for the stunning design and Sophie Storr for the outstanding production.

There's no point printing a book if no one reads it, though, which is why I'm indebted to the dynamic Laura Hough and Dani Wilson in sales, the irrepressible Sarah MacMillan in PR and marketing, and the unstinting Eve Wersocki Morris in publicity. And speaking of dynamism, irrepressibleness, and unstintingitivity thanks too to my personal publicist Clair Dobbs at CLD Communications, and Rosie Robinson who runs my social media.

I wouldn't have written any fiction if it hadn't been for the encouragement of my inspirational literary agent Luigi Bonomi: Luigi, thank you for convincing me to take the plunge as an author, and for your ever-oscillating roles as swimming instructor and lifeguard. Thanks, too, to my outstanding acting agent Samira Davies and her equally outstanding team at Independent: Lisa Stretton, Geri Spicer, and Alice Burton.

This book was written in lockdown in Marrakesh, where a short holiday with the van Cutsem family turned into something more like a Haight-Ashbury commune. Rose, Hugh, Grace, Rafe, and Charlie, your humour, adventurousness, and mischievous sense of fun is printed on every page of this book. Enough said. What goes on in 'kesh, stays in 'kesh ... Thanks, too, to Benedict Yorston, tutor extraordinaire; once you left and online schooling kicked in, we appreciated you more than ever!

And while I'm on the subject of Morocco, we here in the Miller family will be forever grateful to our ever-supportive Ourika 'bubble': Martin and Annie Summers, Lynn Guinness, Richard Annesley, Mark and Maggie Allen, Alex and Maria Peto, Stevie Skinner, Fred and Rosena Charmoy, Robin and Charlotte Scott, and Abel and Kenza Damoussi. Thanks also to the brilliant staff at Villa Dar Zitouna who took such good care of us: Mustapha Elmamoune, Zahira Benaryf, Nadia and Aicha Ait Bella, Elhocien Ouaabed, and Moad Douraid. As lockdowns go, I think we got off pretty lightly …

Finally, writing this book has given me a wave of gratitude to my parents, Mick and Marion Miller, who read me so many different fairytales from so many different cultures when I was too young to appreciate how lucky I was. There is magic in fairy stories, way beyond the power wielded by witches and their familiars. If there's any of it here, it's thanks to them.

Turn the page to read an extract from
Ben Miller's first magical adventure . . .

'A sheer delight for kids both big and Small'
Ruth Jones, Award-winning writer and comedian

The
Night I Met
Father
Christmas

The bestselliing author actor and comedian
BEN MILLER

Once, a very long time ago, there was a town near the North Pole, which was home to most of the world's elves. For as long as anyone could remember, almost all of them had worked in the town's shoe factory, which the famous entrepreneurial elf Grimm Grimmsson had built up from scratch.

Elves, as I'm sure you know, are superb shoemakers, using only the very softest leather, which they cut and stitch completely by hand. They are also very good at magic, so each shoe fitted whoever bought it perfectly.

For centuries, no human shoemaker could make a shoe even a tenth as well as elves, so Grimm Grimmsson had no competition. But then humans invented machines that could make shoes almost as quickly and almost as well as those the elves made. Of course, the shoes which human machines made didn't magically fit your foot, but no one cared because they were really, really cheap.

Over time, humans started to forget all about elf shoes, and only bought ones made by machines. Soon, Grimm Grimmsson found it was costing more to run the factory than he was making from selling the shoes and – in a notorious scandal – he left the town in the middle of the night with his shoemakers' pension fund.

All the elves that had worked in the shoe

factory suddenly found themselves out of work overnight. With no wages to feed their families, and nothing for them to do, they soon began to lose heart. Eventually there were two kinds of elf in the town: rich and poor. Which brings me to the main character in my story, Torvil Christmas.

Torvil was most definitely one of the town's rich elves. In fact, as owner of its only toyshop, he had done rather well for himself. But whereas most people who make money are happy to share it with their family and friends, Torvil kept his fortune all to himself.

To be fair, Torvil had no family, and he had no friends. Raised in an

orphanage, he'd never known his mother and father, and had never really been close with anyone his whole life. Our story begins when Torvil was five hundred and six, long past the age when most elves settle down and start a family. Torvil, however, was still very much alone.

(By the way, elves generally live ten times as long as humans. They are considered to be babies until the age of ten, toddlers until the age of thirty, children until they are one hundred and twenty, teenagers until they are two hundred, and grown-ups at the age of three hundred and three.)

Not that Torvil seemed to mind being alone. Money, he'd discovered, could easily take the place of people. And the great thing about money was that it never let you down. If you counted up your fortune after breakfast, you could be sure that it would still be there when you counted it after lunch, and again when you counted it after supper, and again when you counted it one last time before you went to bed. People might come and go, but money was for ever. All you had to do was make sure you didn't spend any of it.

Not spending money was one of Torvil's favourite hobbies. There were no two ways about it: Torvil was *mean*. If an elf came into his shop looking to buy his son or daughter a birthday present, and was too poor to afford any of the beautiful toys, Torvil never helped them out by dropping his prices, or by slipping a pack of *Star Wars* cards into the elf's satchel when he wasn't looking.

'Please, Mr Christmas, show some kindness,' the customer would say, to which Torvil always made the same reply: 'Kindness, my good sir, doesn't pay my bills.'

Now, you might think that having Christmas as his actual surname would have made Torvil a big fan of the festive season, but you'd be wrong. Torvil really didn't like Christmas at all; he hated it. Every Christmas he could remember had been miserable, spent on his own in his empty, cold house, with no friends or family to visit, and without so much as a single Christmas card, let alone a present. As a result, everything that normal people love about Christmas really got on Torvil's nerves: Christmas trees, Advent calendars, people being nice to one another on public transport; all of them put him in a very bad mood indeed.

The only thing that Torvil *did* like about Christmas was the money he made. In fact – and I'm ashamed to tell you this – when Christmas was coming, and every elf in town was scrimping and saving to buy toys, Torvil would put his prices up! His was the only toyshop in town so no one had any choice but to pay the extra cost. For many of the elf children, whose parents were poor, that meant fewer presents. For some, whose parents were very poor, I'm sorry to say it meant no presents at all.

And that's the way things might have stayed, but for a rather extraordinary turn of events. Events that changed Torvil's life for ever. Events that – as you shall shortly see – changed your life too.

LISTEN TO A WORLD OF WONDER WITH BEN MILLER

ISBN 978-1-4711-9535-8

Actor, comedian and bestselling author
Ben Miller beautifully narrates
his magical new adventure.

Enjoy more captivating audiobooks read by Ben Miller:

ISBN 978-1-4711-7696-8

ISBN 978-1-4711-8548-9

ENTER A
WORLD OF
WONDER

A CLASSIC ADVENTURE FROM BESTSELLING
BEN MILLER

HOW I
BECAME
A DOG
CALLED
MIDNIGHT

The best magic happens when
the clock strikes twelve ...

A magical new adventure
from actor, comedian and bestselling author
BEN MILLER